Night Bird Flying

DANNY SHOT

ROADSIDE PRESS

Night Bird Flying
Copyright ©Danny Shot 2025
Cover Photography: ©D Troeller @ Buzz Photo
ISBN: 979-8-9905466-6-0
Library of Congress Control Number: 2024950272

This is a work of fiction and creative non-fiction. Names, characters, places and incidents are used fictitiously. While the events portrayed in this book are based on reality, some names and identifying details have been changed to protect the privacy of the people involved.

Some of these stories have appeared in one form or another in the following publications: *Long Shot, Evergreen Review, Red Fez, A Gathering of the Tribes, WORKS*

Thank You: Caroline, members of Robert and the Exploding Garbage Can Band (living and dead), Cynthia Ellerington, and The Academy for Teachers

Edited by Michele McDannold
Cover photo by Deborah Troeller
Author photo by John Dalton

Roadside Press
Colchester, IL

Table of Contents

Ich bin ein New Yorker

I live in Hoboken. That's on the Jersey side of the Hudson River. We like to believe we're part of New York. Last week at the fireworks I saw a man wearing a "Hoboken – the 6th Borough" baseball cap. We like to joke that Staten Island is more a part of Jersey than Hoboken is. I'm not just talking geographically. Now, whether you as a New Yorker see me as a fellow native doesn't matter in the least - Ich bin ein New Yorker. Why? Because I said so.

I wish it were like that. Truth is New Yorkers don't see it my way. Even though I was born in the Bronx, and lived a number of years in the East Village, because I have committed the unpardonable sin of living much of my life in New Jersey, I will never be accepted as a New Yorker. Brave souls lucky enough to escape the provinces of Kansas or Kentucky, after a few years of paying dues are welcomed with open arms to the rarefied ranks of New Yorkers. Sting is a New Yorker, Bruce Springsteen is not. Madonna is a New Yorker, Frank Sinatra never was. The only exceptions to the rule as I see it are Allen Ginsberg and Patti Smith, both of whom achieved dual citizen status. Jack Nicholson had to relocate to the West Coast to escape his Jersey roots. Martha Stewart had to thoroughly reinvent herself. Bruce Willis (and John Travolta) will always be Jersey, no matter where he hides.

It really shouldn't matter. But it does. I wear the mantle of Jerseyite proudly enough, but it came at a cost. When I was a young poet living on 12th Street between Avenues A and B in the early 80s, I hung around St. Marks Poetry Project. I always thought I was as good as (better, actually) the other poets my age, but whenever I was introduced at a reading I was introduced as a

Jersey poet, even though I lived in New York and planned on doing so my whole life. Eliot Katz and I published a literary magazine titled *Long Shot,* which often got notice, but usually with the tag "from New Jersey." Often enough the reviewer would mention our "strong working-class sensibilities, muscular poetry and Jersey aesthetic no matter how many poems and illustrations we'd publish by downtown hipsters. One night, high on mescaline, walking down (up?) Houston Street at 3 in the morning, my good friend Rob Press got so mad at me because I let it slip to the girls we were walking with that we were from Jersey. What can I say, I couldn't lie, I was tripping. Needless to say, the girls disappeared soon after my ill-timed words made their way into the ether.

I lived in San Francisco in 1980. My girlfriend and I wanted to practice on a smaller scale city before we settled down for a life of bohemian splendor in Manhattan. I would tell people I was from New York, and I must say, for the most part, the Californians (and pretty much any one from the west) were thoroughly unimpressed. But if I let it slip that I was from New Jersey, a whole other type of response was forthcoming. "Oh, you're from Joisey, huh?" I can unequivocally state that never once in my life did I say Joisey, but to Californians' untrained ears I might as well have just come off the boat from Belleville or Perth Amboy. After some initial teasing, my tormentor would betray a note of awe in their line of questioning. A few people asked if I ever saw anyone killed, and I would usually say "no, not really" not wanting to get into the details of having lost a number of friends to mundane suburban auto wrecks and pill induced overdose/suicides.

Granted, maybe I'm not really a New Yorker, but I'm certainly not a tourist. I'm simply a man with a family. New Yorkers can't seem to grasp this, it's absolutely beyond the pale; a man walking with a wife and two children has to be on vacation. Natives seem willing to accept that a family with a child is possible, but two children immediately register as family vacation. Now if these two children are teenagers, and they happen to be walking with their parents, that's virtually inconceivable to the New York state of mind. Whether stopping for a quick bite at Dojos or picking up my wife Caroline at work above the Shubert Theater, people are always trying to get us onto the dreaded double decker tour buses, or worse, to a comedy show. "Do you like comedy?" My sons know the drill, "No!" I've got nothing against stand-up comedy, but I resent the notion that we are seen as tourists. My two Hoboken born and bred sons are as worldly (if not more) as the New York City high school students I have taught the past 25 years.

Occasionally, while traveling via subway, a well-meaning New Yorker will smile benevolently and ask "where you from?" When I politely reply "Hoboken," they'll say "Oh, that's in New Jersey, my wife's cousin lives in Jersey." This reminds me of *The New Yorker* cartoon/map of the world from a New Yorker's perspective. There's New York, there's Los Angeles, separated by an endless wasteland (signified by Nebraska) of which New Jersey is the western border. It's not like we're a red state or anything. In national and senatorial elections, New Jersey votes Democratic more consistently than New York ever did. Hell, we don't even have Republicans in Hudson County.

New Yorkers, even the most sophisticated view New Jersey as monolithic, as if it's all the same. New Jersey is a series of towns and cities each with its own particular character. While it may be true that Jersey boasts some of the crappiest cities, and some of the tackiest, yet most alluring shore towns in the nation, Jersey City is a far cry from Atlantic City, and Hoboken is a very different place than Short Hills. However, New Yorkers tend to typecast us as wanna be Sopranos. True, James Gandolfini's autographed photo does grace the walls of many a Hoboken pizzeria (not to mention shoe repair shops), but contrary to popular belief, we are not all connected. It's simply that Hoboken takes care of its own, and even its most upstanding citizens are willing to look the other way now and then.

I was raised, for the most part, in Bergen County. I'm not proud of it. As a matter of fact, when I die, I want to be cremated, not because I have an aversion to being buried, but I fear spending the afterlife buried in Paramus New Jersey. You would probably have to have gone to Dumont High School to understand. Dumont is where I grew up; an Irish working-class town about 10 miles north of the Washington Bridge. Relatives, when they would visit, referred to it as "delightfully dumpy Dumont." My mother never accepted the fact that we lived in Jersey. My father who came to the United States from Germany in 1928 and struggled mightily in New York during the Depression, relished Jersey living. My mom would take me into the city at least once a week to visit friends or just to walk around. Sometimes she would take me out of school for the day to go to Radio City or the Metropolitan Museum. My dad and I would go to Washington Heights once a month because it was insanely cheap at the Dominican barber shops, and my dad was never one to miss an opportunity to save a dollar.

In high school my friends and I would go to the City every week (more often in the summer), to the Schaeffer Concerts in Central Park, or Mills Tavern or Grass Roots in the East Village because they had no drinking age policy whatsoever. I was one of the brave ones, the guide who was unafraid of the dangers of the big city. We would go to the same Washington Heights neighborhood where my dad had brought me to get my hair cut just a few years earlier, to buy weed by the half pound, which would get us through the week at Memorial Park where we would hang 6 out of 7 nights of the week. By the time I was 15 years old, my primary ambition in life was to get the fuck out of Dumont, New Jersey. That's why I went to college; Rutgers, the state university.

Enough about Dumont, Hoboken is where I live now. Hoboken is a unique city known for its corruption, Frank Sinatra, and (in our minds) as the birthplace of baseball. It looks like the Bronx or Brooklyn in the 1950s or 60s, so much so that films depicting New York of this era are often shot in Hoboken. *A Bronx Tale* was filmed in Hoboken. We also love elections. We had one just a couple of weeks ago. The new mayor lost the election based on the voting machine tally, but snatched victory from the jaws of defeat when a disproportionate number of write in votes were tallied. But it's okay, because the Governor and Senator supported the new mayor who even though he only has lived in Hoboken for 7 years, captured the born and bred constituency. Mind you, I've lived in Hoboken for over 20 years and I'm considered a newcomer. Truth is, many die hard Hobokenites would consider me a New Yorker.

The town (to New Yorkers it's a town, to Jerseyites it's a city) is basically a square mile, hence the nickname "Mile Square City." It stretches on the Western shore of the Hudson River between the Holland and Lincoln Tunnels, or from a New York perspective between Houston and 18th Streets. At one time, Hoboken claimed the honor of having more bars per square mile than anywhere in the world. In the more recent gentrified era we've dropped to third or fourth place, but needless to say, you can easily find a drink in Hoboken. We have a great rock club in Maxwell's which has hosted bands such as Nirvana, REM, and Sonic Youth and served as the stage for Springsteen's Glory Days video. Maxwell's (like yours truly) suffers the weight of being "from Jersey." A *New York Times* article once stated that Maxwell's was "so New York that it's in New Jersey." What does that mean? Can it apply to me? No matter what anyone in Brooklyn might tell you, Hoboken has the best pizza in the world, and that includes Italy. We also have the biggest slices in the world, with Benny Tudino's, Five Star, and Fillipo's competing for the honors. I'd be willing to wager that we have more nail salons per square mile, but I hear that's a growing trend universally. We may very well also have more real estate brokers than anywhere else. Even though the real estate bubble may have burst across America, every day I see unctuous agents parading anxious well-scrubbed couples through the streets of Hoboken.

There's no place more New Jersey than the 9th Street PATH station at 2:30 on a Saturday morning. Most New Yorkers don't know this place exists; its entrance and exit is a mere square hole carved into an existing building. Walking from the street underground to the train station is like walking through a 3-D windswept H.R. Giger illustration, lots of hoses, wires, and dark rounded corners. The PATH (Port Authority Trans Hudson) system is a small-scale commuter rail line that connects downtown New York to either Jersey City or Hoboken. Real old timers still refer to the PATH as the tubes, but I believe it hasn't been called that in 50 or 60 years. Every few years, the Port Authority, under tremendous pressure from a new New York mayor or governor is forced to raise fares, I suspect to not make the NYC subway system look bad with its ever-escalating fare increases. Of course, with the raised fares comes the promise of improvements and better service. Right.

For the most part, since 9/11 the PATH system has cut service. Somehow, the people who run PATH refuse to acknowledge that people from New Jersey go to the City for fun. Which brings us to 2:30 Saturday morning. Let's be honest – everyone's drunk, except those on drugs. There are no bathrooms in the PATH station. Every few minutes you'll see a drunk stagger to the end of the platform and pee onto the tracks. Nine out of ten times, it's a guy. Occasionally, a uniformed Port Authority police officer will pop out of a stainless-steel door at the end of the station, grab the perpetrator and pull him back behind the stainless-steel door, never to be seen again. But this only happens once or twice a night.

There's not enough benches. While over a hundred drunk and rowdy bridge and tunnelers will be in the station at any time, there's enough bench space for maybe 12 lucky souls. The rest of us sit on the floor, propped up against the tile columns in various states of zombie consciousness. Every now and then we are awakened from our alcohol induced slumber by someone near us vomiting onto the tracks. The Port Authority in its infinite wisdom has weekend service, meaning one train serves both Jersey City and Hoboken. After 12:30, it runs every 40 minutes. Often, the trains are so full that you can't get on and have to wait another 40 minutes. Those with enough presence of mind will get on the train going uptown, take it to 34th Street and then take it back downtown to New Jersey. Spouses returning home moments before sunrise have a built-in excuse in the PATH trains.

Whether it be July or December, the PATH station is usually a temperate 92 degrees and the faint smell of sulfur adds to the overall ambiance. It is not uncommon to see people shedding articles of clothing as if we're all playing a virtual slow-motion game of strip poker. The combination of heat, smell, time passing languorously, and alcohol (or drugs) coursing through our systems, sometimes (like every 15 minutes) leads to temper flare ups. It might be something as simple as "why you staring at my girl?" or as complex as "gimme another cigarette chief" that triggers the row. Usually some pushing and shoving, maybe a few punches thrown, now and then a knife flashed, and then the Port Authority cops come out of the silver door at the end of the platform and arrest the guilty parties. About a year ago, one of the cops accidentally discharged a tear gas canister and we all had to be treated outside. We missed 2 or 3 trains. When I got home at about 5 o'clock, my wife looked at me incredulously as I told her my story. I thought she had to believe me because it was true, but I could tell by the disappointment in her eyes that she thought I reached an unimaginative new low in excuse making.

I am willing to admit that the facts might belie my claims of being a real New Yorker, but I also must present mitigating factors to at least offer the possibility of dual citizenship status. First of all, I pay taxes to New York. Secondly, I'm Jewish, not exactly a model specimen, but a member of the tribe nonetheless, and if my ethnic background will grant me Israeli citizenship, I don't see why it can't allow me New York status. Thirdly, I have opinions about everything, even things I know nothing about, and what's more New York than that? As stated earlier, I was born in the Bronx, off the Grand Concourse, a mere Mickey Mantle's stone throw from Yankee Stadium. It's not my fault that my parents pulled up stakes during my formative years for the seemingly greener pastures of Bergen County, New Jersey.

I have frequently stated the belief that New York City should secede from New York State and along with North Jersey and Long Island should form a new 51st state, but upon reflection, I understand that at this juncture, this notion may be perceived as somewhat self-serving.

When I originally planned on moving to New York in the early 80s, my urban pioneering college friends encouraged me with open arms, with all sorts of plans and adventures awaiting. It wasn't until I had actually moved to the City that my friends found themselves too busy with the sort of things that New Yorkers do to actually hang out with their newly arrived provincial friend from Jersey. I met my wife in New York, even though she originally hailed from Jersey. We worked on the eighth floor of Macy's; she sold crystal, and I manned the China Department. When I tell acquaintances about how we met, they often respond, "Oh, it's like a beautiful Christmas story." I guess to New Yorkers, falling in love (and running off to live happily ever after) on the eighth floor of Macy's, next to Santaland, has to be a Christmas story.

When I met Caroline, my roommate Rob and I lived at 519 East 12th Street in the smallest apartment any two men of any sexual orientation might have shared. The tragedy of the apartment was that we chose it because of the $350 a month rent, when we could have had an apartment of almost twice the size across the street for $400 a month. We chose this block because Allen Ginsberg lived a few buildings down. Our bathtub was in the kitchen which was the main room where I slept. If you sat on the couch and put your feet up, you could rest them on the bathtub. Rob slept in the back bedroom, a bare white walled 10' by 12' room with a high window the size of a 12 inch record album jacket that wouldn't open. There were no closets, so we hung our shirts and jackets on the shower frame, which we would have to remove for those occasions we wanted to shower. When Caroline and Rob's girlfriend of the month would stay over, it was a cozy living situation indeed. Somehow, we had parties, usually after bar closing time in which we could jam

10 to 12 inebriated souls into the confines of our East Village bachelor pad.

It was from this vantage point that I began my career as an English teacher in New York City public high schools. I began at Automotive High School in Williamsburg Brooklyn in 1985. This was the time of a great teacher shortage, so I just walked into the Board of Education headquarters in Brooklyn, was fingerprinted and 4 weeks later was standing in front of a class. I was handed a box of chalk, an eraser and given the sage advice, "don't let the bastards near the windows." The students of this illustrious institution had a choice of two majors; Auto Mechanics or Auto Body. You can imagine their interest in Shakespeare. But I learned quickly, and over the years have had a successful career teaching in the South Bronx (Gompers H.S.), Manhattan (A. Philip Randolph H.S. and the Choir Academy of Harlem) and Brooklyn (Tech) again. The way I figure it, over my 25-year career, I have taught over 3,000 New Yorkers who went on to become teachers, professors, doctors, mechanics, traffic cops, chefs, stock brokers, engineers, actors, bartenders, web designers, models, lawyers, electricians, soldiers, and poets. That's got to count for something, right? As much as I might wish to the contrary, there's no denying I'm a Jersey guy. But there's also no denying that I'm a New Yorker too. I've paid my dues.

72 Scars

We all have them. I'd like to say there are two kinds of scars; internal and external, those you can see and those you can't, but upon reflection I'd have to say that there is a limitless variety of scars a body can have. You can fill in the blanks here as to the specific categories of stigmata one can bear because scarring is a very subjective matter. There were at least five types of scars I accumulated during the 1972-73 year. As a point of reference, I should state that I'm Jewish and have been either a student or a teacher for most of my life so my years begin in September. If you include my unspoken unrequited infatuation with Jenny Berman there are six varieties of scars, but that's a topic for another story. My son Levi just asked me what I was writing about and I told him "scars" and he said, "are you writing about your mom's cooking?" OK, I suffered seven varieties of scars in 1972.

I. Acne Vulgaris

Technically speaking, Scar #1 began in 1971 and lasted well into the 1980s. Like many teenagers, I had acne, but unlike many teenagers, I had the worst case any doctor had ever seen. The only thing to compare it to is Charles Bukowski's description in *Ham on Rye*. It started out innocently enough. My dad would drive me to Dr. Fried in Englewood, NJ every Saturday of my freshman year. The treatment would begin with a 30 second x-ray radiation treatment of the afflicted areas and then Dr. Fried would take out a dermatological instrument and go to work squeezing the pimples on my face and back. What I did not know was that Dr. Fried would use the same instrument on all his patients. Within two months I developed a staph infection which resulted in general fatigue, but worse, scabby lesions all over my face, back and chest.

My parents talked about suing the dermatologist for malpractice, but never got around to it. Somehow, I wound up being referred to the 5th Avenue offices of world-famous dermatologist Dr. Norman Ohrentreich. Dr. Ohrentreich was famous for being the inventor of the hair transplant and his clients at the time included hockey player Bobby Hull, Frank Sinatra and U.S. Senator Joe Biden. But I wasn't there for hair plugs, my case of acne/staph infection was so severe, that the good doctor agreed to take my case for free if he could photograph my face and body to illustrate a series of articles for medical journals about the aggressive treatment of acne. You know the saying; publish or perish. My malady included huge boils erupting on an almost daily basis. I'm not talking about your garden variety pimple, but cysts that would spring up between my eyes or on the side of my jaw and disfigure the shape of my face. My torso was so ravaged that my friend Rusty affectionately called me PB for pizza back. The aggressive treatment included large doses of the steroid prednisone and the lancing of each individual boil with a scalpel, or lancet as it was called. This treatment (free though it was) went on for the next decade though high school and college.

Did I mention that the treatment hurt like hell? Sometimes the doctor, or one of his associates had the honor, but usually this regrettable task fell to one of the nurses. In the name of accuracy, I must point out that the Ohrentreich Medical Group had more than its fair share of young pretty nurses. Often, fantasy was the tool of choice for getting through the treatment. I would pretend that I was a captured American pilot being tortured by my nazi captors, but I was loyal to the end never giving any more information than my name, rank and serial number. Of course my mind often wandered off task and I wondered if the nurse would mind at all if I slid my hand up her mini-skirted uniform as she jabbed me with a scalpel. It seemed well within the bounds of reason and fairness. If she simply shed her uniform and lanced my wounds in bra and panties, it definitely would have gone smoother. I think.

One Saturday, Melissa who was my favorite nurse, remarked to one of her assistants, "Note this in the report, 'patient has low pain threshold.'" This was the unkindest cut of all. First of all, I had spent the better part of two years' worth of Saturdays in an intimate state of undress, pain, and arousal with her and she damn well knew my name. Secondly, it really did hurt. The scabs were so thoroughly infected that it would have bordered on intolerable had Melissa touched them with a feather. After this, the doctor came up with a new line of attack: freeze the boils with liquid nitrogen administered in a stumpy syringe (minus the needle) before lancing them. Believe me, the liquid nitrogen was no improvement. It felt as if someone was putting a cigarette out all over my face and body. This treatment went on for years, and a quick look at my face will show the results. To this day. I use beauty products designed for women to minimize the appearance of scarring on my face. It could have been worse. I guess.

I broke up with, no, my girlfriend in college broke up with me because I refused to take my shirt off while we were going at it. I thought she wouldn't want to touch me if she saw the extent of the scarring. Nowadays, if someone comments on my scars, I'll often say something like "there was a fire when I was 15, I don't want to talk about it." This works pretty well because a) I don't have to talk about it, and b) it adds an aura of mystery to a rather mundane set of circumstances.

II.   **Nose**

Three basic activities occupied my time during the summer of 1972. Primarily, I walked or rode my bike around town hoping against hope that I would run into one of the three girls who sat at my lab table in biology. Fantasies of Nan, Christine and Rose occupied a great deal of my waking consciousness, usually involving my heroic rescuing of any which one of them from a truly apocalyptic threat, escaping barely alive but with enough vigor left to engage in round of slow sweaty lovemaking (often in the school bathroom) before departing this mortal coil and passing on to another state of existence. If I had been fortunate enough to run into Nan, Christine or Rose on one of my daily sojourns around town, I don't know what I would have said or done, probably just smile, mumble "hi," and move on. But it was a moot point as these girls were out of my league and out of my horny male pubescent circle of friends.

That summer I also went to the Eastern Track and Field Sports Village somewhere in the wilds of Pennsylvania at the recommendation of my cross-country coach, Mr. Norman Fink. During my freshman year our cross-country team won the New Jersey State Championship. We were a team of about thirty brave, intrepid harriers and I have to admit I was about twenty-fifth best, but nonetheless we all were state champions. If you were to visit Dumont High School today, you would see my name on a plaque on a wall of the Sports Hall of Fame because in 1991(the 20th anniversary of our feat) the team was inducted en masse. But I digress. Back in 1972, our coach suggested that a few of us scrubs go to track camp to learn how to run and to build some muscle.

The other thing I did that summer was learn how to box. The first Ali-Frazier battle had been fought a year earlier and boxing was huge all across America. Dumont Recreation had a summer boxing league and I thought, "what the hell, maybe I'd learn to defend myself," so I signed up. Surprisingly, I took to boxing. I didn't like to get hit (because it hurt my acne) which in a way made me a better boxer because I was aggressive punching wildly and quickly so that my opponent didn't have much time to counter against the onslaught. While boxing I was pretty much always 100% in the moment, alert enough to hear my father yelling "keep your guard up, thumbs tucked in." Dad liked to watch me box, I think because it pleased him to see his only son show some measure of toughness in my easy going non-confrontational life. I also danced around a lot, taking to heart Muhammed Ali's motto "float like a butterfly, sting like a bee," so that if my opponent had any hopes of hitting me he'd have to catch me first. Granted, I weighed about 120 pounds soaking wet so most of my opponents were 6th or 7th graders. Through July and August I chalked up an impressive 5-0 record, and in so doing developed a bit of confidence if not exactly a killer instinct. It was August of 1972 that I first recognized the look of fear in another human being's eyes.

I beat everyone in my weight class rather easily. The director of the program figured everyone would be best served if I moved up in weight class and boxed kids my own age. My first match in my new weight class was against Don Palino a kid a year older who tormented me when I was in 7th grade. Don was a weird kid. He moved to Dumont from Virginia as an eighth grader and got the nickname Johnny Reb even though I think he was half Black. At some point during his first year in Dumont, Don brought in to school really dirty pictures that he had stolen from his older sister Mimi's drawer of her naked and playing with herself. These were the first pornographic pictures that any of us had ever seen, and this made Don quite popular with all of us. Don was a really fast runner and he liked to fight. Though he was wiry he thought nothing of taking on any kid in the school. He even got into a fight with Mr. Barlow our none too bright gym teacher during a particularly heated game of slam bang. For some reason, Don hated me, I can't figure out why. To this day I am shocked when I find out that someone, whether it be a student, a fellow teacher, or another writer dislikes happy go lucky me.

I was looking forward to fighting Don, because after all, I was 5-0 and I could hold my own. The bell rang, I put up my guard, and within perhaps a second and a half I saw a gloved fist smash into my nose accompanied simultaneously by a low grunt (Don) and a squishing sound (my nose). If you ever saw *Raging Bull* starring Robert DeNiro, think of the slow-motion fight sequence against Sugar Ray Robinson. From the moment of impact, I saw blood splashing in front of my eyes and onto Don's shirt. I offered a weak left jab that glanced off Don's shoulder and then there were people in the ring including my father. Someone wanted to call an ambulance, but my dad insisted that he would take me to Holy Name Hospital.

My broken nose was reset, packed and bandaged. When he

came into the emergency room, I noticed how pale and shaken my dad looked. Later that night, as I lay in bed I heard my mom scolding him about how she "wanted an end to this foolishness." About a week later I ran into Rose at Uncle Franks Pizza and she wanted to know why the black eye and all the bandages. I explained that I broke my nose boxing at Dumont Rec. "Poor thing," was all she offered. By the third week in September Rose was Don's steady girlfriend.

III.   **Heel**

Eastern Track and Field Sports Village was a camp where some of the best high school athletes from New Jersey, New York and Pennsylvania went to hone their skills. I wasn't one of them, but I learned a few tricks that made me a better runner. It's also where I got Plantars Warts on both my heels. Plantars warts might not sound like the most debilitating injury to beset a young man, but coupled with my staph infection, they turned into mini cauliflower shaped growths that took over the entire heel of each foot. I couldn't walk.

At the beginning of September, I went to Englewood Hospital for the surgical removal of the Plantars Warts. The doctor used a surgical instrument that looked like an apple corer that dug a hole about the size of a penny from the surface of the heel all the way to the bone. I was on crutches through September and had to walk with a cane until Christmas. My cross-country season was over before it began. Same with track. Between my staph infection, broken nose, broken thumb, and disabled feet I missed the entire year of gym.

I still have scars on each heal though they are hard and callused over. On certain days when I am tired after a long day of work or of walking, they will throb with a dull pain that moves up my calves, knees and thighs causing leg weariness I will pay Levi two dollars a foot to massage them with the emphasis on the heels. My wife shakes her head and sucks her teeth at my apparent self-indulgence, but I think it's a good way for my son to earn a few quick bucks. About once a year I'll splurge and go to China-town for an hour session of reflexology.

IV.   **Thumb**

Johnny Eager died on Wednesday October 18, 1972. When talking about those days, I sometimes exaggerate and call Johnny Eager my best friend. He wasn't really. But he was a good friend. I'll also call him my guardian angel. He was. Is. John lived across the street and over two houses at 28 Forest Road. He had two older brothers, one of whom was on his second tour of duty in Vietnam and another who was rumored to be a junky who was not allowed to set foot in Dumont or he would be shot. John was one of, if not *the* coolest kid in town. He played drums in various bands in the area and the girls loved him. He liked to say "I'm a lover, not a fighter," but nothing could be farther from the truth. John loved to fight. One of the reasons I got involved with boxing was because John went. He was sort of a hippie, he had long hair, he smoked pot, but more so he was an old-fashioned greaser. He loved to rumble, and he loved his car.

Those of us who lived on Forest Road hung out at Bedford Park. In suburban New Jersey we didn't have gangs, but we had parks. A park was your home turf and one's park was to be de-fended at all costs. What park you hung out at was determined by where you lived, and where you lived was determined by your parent's social class. Pretty much all of Dumont was Irish or Italian working class, yet there were still different economic stra-ta. For some reason, the older greasers liked to come to Bed-ford Park and terrorize us younger hippies. I remember greasy Frankie Haddolin pulling up in his GTO, getting out clutching a pair of hedge clippers and chasing my friend Rusty threatening to cut his hair so he looks like a man. On mischief night they would chase us with cans of Nair and tube socks filled with ce-ment instead of flour. You don't want to know what they called Willy Rose, the only Black kid our age in Dumont.

John was the King of Bedford Park. He may have been a greaser, but he was by no means averse to fighting other greasers. As a matter of fact, he relished the opportunity. Needless to say, John was the sort of person you wanted to stay on the good side of. We spent much time flattering him and always shared our liquor and pot. John carried drumsticks in his back pocket, and on occasion would use our heads as a drum kit, but we never minded. Anyone between the ages of 8 and 18 who lived on our block or hung out at Bedford Park was safe. All it took was a word, and John was on it. He would drive through town, and before he could drive, ride his bike looking for the perpetrators. If his efforts were fruitless, he would settle on someone who was friends with the offending party and beat the shit out of him. Johnny Eager was a good friend to have. After his death, none of our lives were the same and old scores were settled with a vengeance.

He died when the car he was driving on an upstate beer run smashed into a telephone pole on Route 303. He and his two passengers were killed instantly. We found out about it the next day in school. After the Vice Principal announced the tragedy over the loudspeaker, the entire school fell into a state of shock. About a minute after the announcement, I bolted out of home-room and ran to the bathroom. I locked myself in a stall and cried like a baby. After a few minutes I pulled myself together. As I was leaving, I punched the door with all my might catch-ing my thumb between the door and the frame. I didn't feel a thing. It was Nan who asked me during 5th period lunch what was wrong with my hand. My thumb was purple and bent at an odd angle behind the back of my hand. Nan walked me to the nurse's office; my dad was called and he drove me to Englewood Hospital to get my thumb set and put in a splint. My parents let me take the next two days off from school. Walking with a cane is not all that difficult. Walking with a cane with a broken thumb is a challenge indeed.

V.   Heart

That night I had the strangest dream. I dreamt that Rusty and I went to Johnny Eager's funeral at Frech Funeral Home in Du-mont. I was wearing a velvet suit. Many of the kids from school were there. All of Bedford Park was there. Teachers were there. But many members of my extended family were there as well. My Brother-in-Law Leo was there. So were his parents, Paul and Bronia. Uncle Kurt and Aunt Elizabeth. My sister Carol's best friend Ann. "What are you doing at Johnny Eager's funeral?" I asked each individual. The answer was always the same "I'm here to pay my respects."

My father died on Friday, October 20th. I'd like to say that it started out as a normal day, but I can't. Since I had the day off from school, I slept until about 9 in the morning. When I woke up, Dad was still sleeping. He had retired in September after working 30 plus years as a machinist at Bendix (an aerospace company). When I was little, I marveled how anyone could have a job where they had to get up at 6 in the morning. When he came home around 4:30 he would take an hour nap before dinner and I would often fall asleep next to him. I usually got up at 7 on school days and since his retirement Dad was always at the kitchen table to greet me. As a matter of fact, he was my alarm clock. So it was odd that he was still sleeping. I wanted to wake him, but Mom said "Shh let him rest, he's been so tired lately."

At lunchtime, I hobbled to the front gate at school and talk-ed a few of my friends into cutting the afternoon and going to the McGovern rally in Hackensack. Dad drove Mom, me, Rusty, Phil and Dave to the event in front of the county court-house which was packed with thousands of supporters, includ-ing many teenagers who had cut school to be part of history. George McGovern spoke sensibly and eloquently to thunderous applause. After he was done speaking, my father leaned into me, "He's going to do it. I can feel it, he can win."

At 5 o'clock we went to Johnny Eager's wake. I fought with my parents about what I was going to wear, but in the end, I pre-vailed and went in a flannel shirt and jeans. We hung around for about 20 minutes, my parents joining the adults from the neighborhood and me joining my friends from Bedford Park. Before leaving, I paid my respects at the open coffin. Johnny didn't look real, he looked like a figure at a wax museum. I had never seen a dead body before. Neither of my parents came up to the casket.

At about 9:15 my mother and I were in her room watching *Love American Style* when we heard a thump in the kitchen. After asking each other "what was that," but not really wanting to look until the commercial break, I went to see what the noise was. Dad was on the floor, sort of in the fetal position. I yelled "Dad wake up!" but he didn't move. I kept yelling before shaking him but all I heard was a rattling sound, sort of like snoring but coming from his throat. His eyes were open but unseeing and his skin was cold. Mom came in and she started screaming "No! No! as I tried to get Dad back in his chair. I knew he was dead, but I thought I had to try to make him alive, somehow. Mom called an ambulance, and then my sister and brother-in-law (Carol and Leo) who lived 3 blocks away. The ambulance and Carol and Leo arrived at the same time. I watched as they pumped his chest and applied the electricity to no avail. They eventually gave up and covered him with a sheet as we waited for a doctor to come and pronounce him dead.

By this time, the entire block was outside standing in front of our driveway in the flashing ambulance light. My mother and sister were in the living room hugging each other and crying. Leo and I went into the driveway to tell the neighbors. "What happened? Is everything okay?" Neither Leo nor I knew what to say. Finally I blurted out "My dad's dead. He just died." A low murmur filled the crowd followed by an "Oh my God." I think it was Mrs. Eager. Then people started hugging each other and crying and for some reason I decided right then and there that I wouldn't cry. I just stood there alone not knowing what to do or say. Finally, Judy Conti the older girl who lived next door came to me and hugged me tightly while sobbing hysterically. I held her and told her "It's gonna be okay. It's gonna be okay. It's gonna be okay." My mantra for the rest of the night.

The funeral was on Sunday, October 22, 1972 at the Gutterman Musicant Funeral Parlor in Hackensack followed by burial at Beth-El Cemetery in Paramus. I wore a blue velvet jacket, a white shirt and black slacks. It was just like my dream, with pretty much the same cast of characters, but this time I didn't have to ask anyone "what are you doing here?"

Postscript. My cat Bootsy died on November 20, 1972, one month after my father. I woke up and petted my cat who usually found his way into my bed sometime in the night. He was cold and stiff. Just dead. I wanted to cry but didn't.

On November 7, 1972 Richard Nixon defeated George McGovern in the largest landslide in election history.

It's gonna be okay.

And We Drown...

"I want Susie DeSalvo," Dusty screamed as he crawled across our gym teacher's lawn. Mr. McKinley was a mean motherfucker who just returned from 'Nam convinced that us suburban Jersey boys were sissies. McKinley's solution to any disobedience in class was to pull out the gloves and stage an impromptu boxing match, always with predictable results.

"Shut the fuck up, and let's get out of here," I shout as I pull Dusty by the collar. My parents were away and Dusty, Billy and I had raided the liquor cabinet and drank a quart of Old Grand-dad. Billy was already in the hospital. At Bedford Park, we saw a couple sitting on a bench. Billy sat down between them and started kissing the girl, Rose who was in our Personal Development class. Personal Development was an "optional class" for intelligent misfits, miscreants and general fuck-ups. The guy, Frankie, one of Dumont's greasers took an immediate dislike to Billy and punched him straight in the throat. Billy fell to the ground making gurgling noises. Frankie took Rose by the hand and stepped over Billy's body pausing to step on his head with his Durangos. By this point Billy's Adams apple had disappeared and lodged itself in his throat. He turned pale blue. Dusty ran to a house near the park and an ambulance was called. Billy was taken to Holy Name Hospital clutching his throat. Dusty and I went back to the basement to drink more whiskey.

Now Dusty was acting up, kneeling on our gym teacher's lawn, arms outstretched to the heavens yelling obscenities. "Come on out McKinley and fight like a man, you shell-shocked bastard." Bring your wife out because when I'm done with you, I'm going to fuck her right here on your front lawn." Every light in every house on Barbara Road was lit except for McKinley's. Dusty kept at it with a suicidal determination.

"What'd you do in Nam, give blowjobs behind the barracks? Why'd my brother have to die so a bastard like you could return to make our lives miserable?"

McKinley's bedroom light went on. I dragged a garbage can from the curb and brought it down on Dusty's head as hard as I could. Dusty looked at me with a crooked smile and then slumped to the ground. Sirens were wailing in the distance. McKinley was at the door in his underwear. I dragged Dusty into the Bedford Park woods and left him to sleep it off.

2.

"The sun always shines at night when you're high," I said to Dusty as we took another pill. "Don't stare at it or it will burn your retinas," I warned.

Dusty lowered his eyes. "You know man, I want to get out of this shithole town with its little people. I feel so damn big sometimes," he said with conviction.

"Yeah," I agreed, "soon we'll be out of school and free of Dumont forever."

"No man, you don't understand, I mean that little town down there." Dusty stopped and pointed with his toe to a tiny anthill in the parking lot. "The little ones don't like me because I'm different. Well fuck them man!" With that Dusty lowered his foot on the anthill and kicked sand about in a psychedelic frenzy. "Wow man, I showed them."

3.

It was a dull night at Memorial Park and the gang had no plans so we smoked some angel dust. Pete and Joe were still bored, but more content with the Teenage Wastelandedness of it all. At about 10:00, a caravan of fast looking cars pulled into the parking lot. The teenagers who piled out of the cars were unbelievable, looking as if they just stepped off the set of *American Graffiti*. Pete and Joe were standing at the edge of the Dumont gang who were moving in on the Cliffside greasers who were talking about a gang war on some neutral turf to the stoned and bewildered Dumont boys.

"Those douchebags," said Pete through clenched teeth, "what right do they have bringing their bad trip to us?" With a war hoop that would have scared the pants off the most hardened vet, he lifted an overflowing steel trash container over his head and marched up the hood of a metallic blue Cliffside Camaro and proceeded to smash it through the windshield.

All hell broke loose. The Dumont forces attacked and began pounding the Cliffside cars with anything that could be found. The greasers were lost. They tried to get back to their cars, but to do so they had to run the gauntlet of crazed Dumont boys. By the time the police arrived, the greasers' cars were wrecked and had to be towed out of town. For once, the cops were on the Dumont hippies' side. The Cliffside greasers were arrested for rioting and disorderly conduct and their parents were called to take them home. After this incident, Dumont developed a reputation as a tough town. We lived it up for all it was worth.

4.

"Quack, quack, quack, quack, quack, quack, quack."
Why is that penguin quacking at me? Do penguins quack?
"Quack, quack, quack, opium, quack, quack, China, missionaries, quack, quack, Dean? Quack, quack, Boxer? Quack, quack, quack."

Shit it's Mr. Allocco. He's not a penguin. Why's he wearing a penguin suit? No, that's just a suit. He's asking a question. The class is laughing, showing their incisors. Jenny Berman looks concerned. She is an angel. I love her. Look at her smile, beatific. She's the only one brave enough to have Bowie hair. Her eyes glisten. I want her more than anything.

"Dean? Dean?"
"Imperialism," I shout all too stridently.
Mr. Allocco looks bewildered. "Exactly."
Vow to self: no more acid during the school day.

5.

"Va-un, Joe."
"Really? Va-un? I don't believe you."
"For real. I did it. Va-un."
"You're lying."
"I wouldn't lie about that" (yes I would).
"With who then?"
"Margaret Cassidy."
"Charlie's going to kill you."
"Charlie's in California. He doesn't have to know."
"Charlie's going to kill you."

Joe and I speak in phone code, an intricate system of one-sylla-ble sounds in Spanish and English we invented so our parents don't know what we're talking about. Va-un means getting laid, or the potential for getting laid, which until tonight were one and the same. Va-dos A (pronounced Ah) means somebody's got weed. Va-dos B (pronounced Bay) means we're going to stand in front of the liquor store on Grant Avenue until some hapless older guy agrees to buy us booze. It usually takes about 10 minutes, but it has been known to take as long as 40.

Charlie is the foreman at the perfume factory. Was the fore-man. That's where we work. Joe and I. It's the only place that hires 15-year-olds. They pay us a dollar seventy-five an hour to stand in line and fill bottles with scented liquid. Actually, the older kids work with the machines, Joe and I stick labels to the bottles. Three labels; *Oh de Paris*, *Black Velvet*, and *Risqué*, three bottle shapes, but the same musky scent in each bottle. Margaret is Charlie's girlfriend. She's 17, but was left back so she's only a year ahead of me in school. She's light years ahead maturity wise. She's a woman.

Last week Charlie and I were sitting in his car getting high when he told me that he was going on an extended trip and to keep an eye on Margaret for him. The next day, when he was picking up the factory payroll at the bank, Charlie just kept on going. He got on a plane for Los Angeles and flew away. A warrant was issued for his arrest but he was gone. Most of the guys were pissed that Charlie took our paychecks but I was happy for him. There's no future in Dumont for an 18-year-old dropout. I was sort of honored that he trusted me to watch Margaret. Then I started thinking — why me? What makes me safe with his girl-friend? Who, or what does he think I am?

I always liked Margaret. Last year she sat next to me in Spanish. She wasn't too good at it but I helped her as best I could. We had a running joke where I would slap the side of my head and exclaim "albondigas, no te dijé" at the slightest provocation. This cracked her up every time. Once she wrote "FREE LOVE FOR A FREE WORLD" in black marker on my jeans. I was in ecstasy for the 20 minutes it took her. Charlie is going to kill me.

It took two bottles of Strawberry Hill to get Margaret where I wanted her. Honestly, I drank more than my fair share. We were talking about her joining Charlie in California at the end of the school year and the next thing we were making out on the bench by the basketball court behind Selzer School. One thing led to another, and then we were doing it in the grass of the soccer field. The whole process lasted less than 5 minutes. Actually, it was the best 4 minutes of my life. After we were done, she just lay there. I couldn't tell if it was from pleasure, exhaustion, or she passed out. Margaret opened her eyes: "Charlie's going to kill you!… Kill us." I got her home and left her wobbly on her front porch as I slipped away.

I call Joe.
"Va-un."

6.

The Who came on at 9:30. The Garden crowd stood up and screamed. Dusty stood up, turned his back to the stage, outstretched his arms and yelled mournfully, "Where is The Who? I want The Who."
The people in the vicinity showered Dusty with beer cans and less wholesome refuse.
"Sit down!" Billy yelled.
"Fuck you man," Dusty screamed, "I can't see The Who!"
With a jolt he turned around and sprinted for the edge of the balcony. Billy and I caught him in mid-flight at the edge of the overhang. Dusty was quiet for the rest of the night. He didn't even complain about the ambiguous vibes coming from Billy's third eye.

7.

Bad day. Thank you Alison Steele, just keep talking, do your night bird thing, let me drift off. The day started unraveling at the park. With Lori Boettger's stupid dog. No, it began with Wayne's wacky weed, this weird grass that looks like parsley or oregano, maybe it was parsley, but it was sprayed with some potent shit. We smoked a bowl and the whole world shifted focus. And then out of nowhere that god-damned mutt was on my leg, humping it for all it was worth. No matter what I did, I couldn't shake it. It was attached. I walked around and dragged the dog with me, everybody laughing, Lori doing nothing whatsoever to heel the beast. Tommy Veroni said "look at the faggots, it takes one to know one." Everybody laughed harder. I didn't know what to do, so I slapped the dog with the side of my hand. All was silent and all eyes were on me, as if I just hit a baby or something. The dog too was stunned. For a second, then he sank his teeth into my hand, drawing blood. Finally, Lori pulled him off. I went to my car and sat alone, turning the radio up to full volume.

My car's not much to speak of. It's a 66 Impala that I bought for 40 dollars. The reason I got it so cheap is because it was hit by a garbage truck and the fender over the rear tire is twisted at an improbable angle. But it's my car, and the radio works. Wayne offered Billy a Quaalude if he would kick in the door on the driver's side with me sitting inside. I'm not much of a fighter, but after the first kick I was face to face with Billy swinging wildly. He was surprised that I was punching him as if I had betrayed our friendship. Fuck him. Fuck all of Memorial Park. I need to stop, or at least slow down.

After I drove off, the ghouls turned their attention to Jenny Berman. So I've been told. Kris, Jason and Pete started calling her a cock tease and a skank. I don't know what she did to raise their ire. Pete told me that when he fucked her, she was like a dead fish, just zoned out of her mind not moving or responding in any way. I don't think I believe him. If I were fucking her, she would be moving and moaning and holding on tight. Anyway, after calling her all sorts of names the boys threw snowballs at her and Darlene, her new friend from Bergenfield. They left the park ahead of a barrage of snowballs from the boys and taunts from the girls. I got to get out of this place. I got to get out of Dumont if it's the last thing I ever do.

8.

Dusty and I spent 6 hours sitting on the couch in my living room. We had taken two hits of windowpane acid. It seemed a harmless enough amount at the time.

Dusty was sitting at a strange angle, his pupils the size of nickels, staring into space. He did not move. Not a sound. Perhaps he was still breathing, but he appeared to be in a true state of suspended animation. I fed him orange juice, but it dribbled down his chin. I yelled in Dusty's ear but there was no response. I slapped him in the face, but he did not blink.

It started four hours earlier while we were watching *Don Kirschner's Rock Concert* on tv. Sparks, a funny looking band, with a guy with a Hitler moustache was playing funny sounding music.

"Dusty," I asked innocently enough, "wouldn't it be funny if your parents were watching the same show and through our television could see us sitting here high as kites on my couch listening to this funny music. The suggestion became instant reality for Dusty. He decided he had to call his mom and apologize for taking drugs, but that he was safe and would soon be back to normal as long as he stayed away from mirrors. I did not think a call home was a prudent course of action.

Every time that Dusty would get up and go near the phone, I would pull him away. For over two hours, the psychodrama played out taking on epic proportions: good versus evil, logic versus ignorance, reason versus emotion, right versus might. I put an end to the battle when Dusty went to the bathroom, disconnecting the phone and hiding it under the kitchen sink. After Dusty came out of the bathroom, I went in and spent an interminable amount of time watching my day-glow urine splash around the toilet. Dusty was on the couch sitting at a forty-degree angle staring off into the cosmos.

I spent the next four hours trying to bring Dusty back. I could see into Dusty's mind. It was blank. At about four thirty in the morning, Dusty blinked: "What did you say?"
I was overjoyed.
Dusty stretched his arms, "Wow man, if you could see what I just saw."
"I did Dusty, I did."
"I'm scared."
"The worst part is over, go to sleep."
We worked for a foul tempered landscaper named Rob. Work started at 7 a.m.
"Dusty, I don't think we should go to work today."
It's okay. I'm better now. Everything is clear."
"Acid has a way of sneaking up on you when you least expect it. I don't think we should go."
"Really, it's okay. I can handle it."
"Well, just don't fuck up."

We lay in our beds quietly for the next hour. I stared at the patterns in the ceiling. At six, we got out of bed, got dressed and walked across town to work.

Rob was waiting for us, frowning, ready to go. He had little styrofoam cups of coffee for us. I tasted mine and immediately spit it all over Rob's driveway. Rob gave me a dirty look. Dusty and I got into the back of the truck. Dusty looked at Rob.
"Rob?"
"Yes, Dusty?"
"Rob, can I ask you a question?"
"Sure."
"Rob, why is your third eye staring at me?"
Damn, Dusty had blown it. I burst out laughing. Rob glared at me.
"What's so funny?"
"Nothing Rob, nothing."
"If you don't like working for me, you can go home right now."
"I'm sorry Rob."
Dusty smiled at Rob, all charm. "Rob?"
"Yes Dusty?"
Dusty made a peace sign. "Lightly salted draperies, man, and watch out for speed bumps."

Rob shook his head, got behind the wheel and we were off. Work was awful. I spent most of the day following Dusty with my lawnmower, straightening out the intricate patterns he had cut into people's lawns. At the end of the day, Rob gave me a lecture about working too slowly and time being money. On Monday, I was demoted to weeding. A week later I quit.

9.

I want to die. Want to die, die, die. How am I going to show my face on Monday? Oh God why, why, why did I ask Donna Maravilla out. She's out of my league, what was I thinking? Maybe because of that time last year when Cathy Triggiani was getting married in St Mary's and we had just gotten high and we wandered into the church and it was beautiful and it smelled like the presence of God and Donna sat next to me and held my hand during the I dos. Then we went back to her house and raided the medicine cabinet for pills and listened to Neil Young and we were wasted and she put her feet in my lap and let me massage them and it was heavenly.

That was last year. In the past 12 months she got more beautiful and curvy while I just got more pimply and then she started going out with Hoagie who's in college and we drifted apart since she's not in college prep classes. A few weeks ago I was talking to her in front of the 7-11 and I just came right out and asked her: "Would you go see the Grateful Dead with me at Roosevelt Stadium?" I originally was going to ask Jenny, but she got shipped away to a foster home after she ran away again. After maybe 10 seconds of thoughtful looking consideration Donna said, "Sure, why not, it'll be fun." So we were on.

I don't really like the Grateful Dead; as a matter of fact, I sort of despise them. I'm more of a Sabbath, Zep sort of guy but stoner girls seem to love the Dead. Joe drove me, Donna and Dusty to the wilds of Jersey City to see the Dead. As everyone knows Roosevelt Stadium is a sewer. Literally, the bathrooms back up and you have to wade ankle deep through the piss to get out. And the whole crowd is wasted; sometimes it gets ugly. After the Allman Brothers show people ripped the seats from the stands and burned them in bonfires in the middle of the field. When I saw Eric Clapton there he was so wasted he only played a ukulele, and cursed at the crowd asking us if we were Satan's children. The Dead was going to be different. All day it drizzled lightly, still the ground was soaked. I had filled my wineskin with Ripple Red in honor of the occasion and Joe had rolled 4 humongous joints.

The Dead was supposed to go on at 3 in the afternoon but I guess because of the rain they didn't start till 4:30. By that time we had smoked all four joints and gone through two wine skins. Then they came on. The crowd erupted. Midway through the first song, "Casey Jones," the guy sitting next to me handed me a pipe of something. I took a deep hit, held it in, felt it coarse through my lungs and then vomited all over Donna Maravilla, a horrible red wine torrent of unremitting nausea. She just looked down in horror, stupefied by my ultimate bad manners. All I could say was "I'm sorry, I'm so so sorry."

Wouldn't you know it, the Dead went on to play a tortuous 5 hour set, lazily meandering through a 40 minute jam of a song called "St. Stephen" about some Christian saint who was tortured, stoned, shot full of arrows, suffered mightily and seemed to somehow get off on it before he died. I was in hell. On the way back home, I mercifully fell asleep in the back seat as Donna squeezed into the front with Dusty and Joe. I'm glad I was passed out so I didn't have to hear them talk. Do I call Donna tomorrow and apologize? Or do I just wish it all away? Maybe if I'm lucky I'll just die in my sleep.

10.

I've got to find friends my own age. Roger and Mike will graduate in a few months and Woody and Murph are old enough to drink legally. Hell, Roger looks like he's been old enough to drink for the past 3 years; he had a Fu Manchu when I met him. I think they let me hang around because I amuse them. And because we can smoke in my room with no parental interference. And because of how many girls I know.

Thank God for Alison Steele's voice to soothe me through my troubles. I hate New Year's Eve. Last year I spent it cradled in the lap of a bus driver vomiting in my seat of the 167 coming back from the City. Tonight wasn't as bad, but still pretty awful. The five of us piled into Woody's car to a party in Teaneck at Fairleigh Dickinson, at the house of some college girl who was in Woody's class. I was clearly the youngest person there and I felt it from the get go. Then Murph started in with this ridiculous story that we were scouts for Warner Brothers Records. Why would he say such a thing to a bunch of college kids? I made less than a minimal attempt to play along and this pissed Murph off. Over the course of 5 or 6 rum and cokes and 7 or 8 tokes of passed around joints, I was feeling pretty good, not wasted, just good. My chief concern was to find someone to kiss at the stroke of midnight. But that wasn't happening. I felt like somebody's tag along kid brother at a grown-up college party. That wasn't so bad. Could have been worse.

At about one, I knew it was time to leave. I looked for my friends, but they were nowhere to be found. I looked across the street and Woody's car was still parked across the street. Thank God. I went outside and Woody and Roger were inside the car. Passed out. I banged on the roof of the car. No response. I hit it harder. Nothing. I shook the car and yelled. Absolutely nothing. Were they that wasted? Or dead? Or did they simply want to be rid of me so much that they were pretending to be unconscious so they could ditch me? Fuck them, I'd get home on my own.
I got onto Teaneck Road and stuck out my thumb. It was bitter cold. Where were my gloves? Shit. After about 20 minutes a guy in a steel gray Range Rover pulled up. He was wearing driving gloves. Who really wears driving gloves?
"Where you headed?"
"Dumont," I told him.
"Get in," he said, "I'm going the same way."
"Thank you. I need the ride."
"How'd you wind up alone on New Year's?"
"It's a long story," I said. "I won't bore you."
"No really, why you alone?"
"It's a long story," I repeated.
At that point right in front of the Diner by Foster Village he lunged at me. I jumped out of the way and out the door. He caught me by my front hip but I pulled away and jumped out. Unfortunately, I don't carry my stuff in a wallet. I carry it in a leather tooled Marlboro cigarette case. He knocked it right out of my pocket and into the night as a wicked gust of wind picked up and scattered the contents through the frigid air. I walked home the remaining two and a half miles.

Again, a prayer of thanks to Alison Steele, the Night Bird, the redeemer of wayward souls. Tomorrow is a new year.

11.

"You guys are pussies! You're scared cause you know I can beat you," said Dusty.

"It's not good to go swimming in this condition. Opium fucks your system up but you don't know it. You can forget to breathe or something," Billy said patiently.

"Anyhow, you can't swim Dusty," I added.

"I can so swim. I'll bet each of you five bucks I can beat you to the other side of the lake. What's the matter, you chicken?"

"Bet!"

Billy was a good swimmer. He made it across the lake in about 5 minutes. I was an average swimmer. By the time Billy reached the other shore, I was half way across. I looked back to where Dusty was. All I could see was his long frizzy hair, then his mouth.

"Help me man, I can't breathe."

A lifeguard in a rowboat paddled around the lake serenely. Dusty addressed his panic to the lifeguard. "Help man, I don't think you understand… I'm drowning." Dusty's head went under again. The lifeguard smiled pleasantly.

"I'm drowning… Dean… save me…"

I was about 200 yards in front and hated the idea of having to turn back. By the time I got to Dusty he had been under water for about a minute and was totally motionless. The only way that I found him was by spotting the mop of hair floating near the top of the water. I was exhausted. I grabbed the hair and began swimming towards shore. I was startled by a powerful whack to the back of my head. Dusty was alive, and crazed. He scratched my neck, pummeled my head, and bit me. Dusty showed teeth I didn't know humans had. It took every bit of strength to make it to the shore.

Billy and I made Dusty pay us before we let him eat that night. When Dusty's steak fell into the fire, Dean and I decided that he couldn't have any more opium. We smoked the rest that night. About 60 dollars worth. Dusty didn't talk to either of us for a week.

12.

I saw Jenny last night. It was beautiful. It was tragic. I'm in love. A whole gang of us went to Oradell Reservoir for an end of the school year swimming bonfire party. There must have been 50 of us. This time the cops didn't take our clothes and make us get out of the water like they did last year. They hadn't arrested anyone, but they sure enjoyed the eyeful they got from lining up us naked teenagers. That was last year.

Last night, sometime around 8, Jenny was there. She had run away from her halfway house in Paramus and was back with us, smoking hash and sitting right next to me by the fire. I didn't know what to say other than "How're you doing? I missed you." Before she could respond, bright lights flooded the clearing and loudspeakers were informing us not to move. Everyone scattered in different directions. Jenny led me by the hand about 100 yards away to some dense bushes. We hid ourselves as best we could staying as quiet as possible. We heard the cops grabbing various people and marching them off. Miraculously, they did not come near our bush. I held Jenny's hand in fright and anticipation. We stayed huddled under the bush for what seemed like an eternity. Slowly I gathered the courage to kiss her. She responded by kissing back. Hallelujah! I was in heaven. After a few minutes I gained the courage to reach under her shirt and touch her breast. No bra. Double Hallelujah!! Jenny is not big breasted;

she sort of resembles Bonnie from the Trots and Bonnie comic strip in *The Lampoon*. I should mention that I've always had a crush on Bonnie. I grabbed a fuller hold. Just then, a blinding light was in my eyes. They found us. We were rousted out of the bushes and pulled apart. The cops weren't interested in me. It was Jen they were after. She was put in a car and driven off. I was left to walk home; they just didn't seem to care about me.

I wonder how I'll see Jenny again. They'll probably move her to another halfway house further away. I'll find a way.

13.

"I left it on the roof of your car, and you drove off."
"Sorry Dusty, I didn't know it was there."
"That was 200 dollars of pharmaceutical."
"I'm sorry, you shouldn't have left it there."
"Let's go back and look for it."
"Dusty, we drove 90 miles today."
"You owe me 200 dollars man."
"Dream on."
"Fuck you."
I got in my car. Dusty tried to hold the door, but I pulled out. I got to get out of this place.

What a Wonderful World

She is the one that I don't want to write about. She is the thing. The one thing I must write about. She is dead now. But that doesn't mean that on occasion my love for her doesn't burn like an ember on a funeral pyre. I don't tell my wife about these feelings. Of course not. Carla is locked away in our collective vault of memory as something that happened long ago, like her barely remembered paintings gathering dust in our overflowing basement. She's put away in the deep folds of my brain with Joey Ramone and Johnny Thunders. Ironically, there's a video on of Joey Ramone singing "What a Wonderful World" and tears are falling from my eyes and I don't know if it's from thinking about Carla or from the "What a Wonderful World" trigger.

Since I'm being uncharacteristically candid, I'll let you in on a personal secret. I tell anyone who might care that I never cry, that I'm incapable of tears. Of course, that's pure egotism on my part. I want people to think I'm hardened, slightly damaged, and mysterious in some inexplicable way. But there are 3 triggers that make me cry every encounter. 1) Lou Gehrig's "today I consider myself the luckiest man alive" speech upon his retirement from baseball in 1939. And yes, Gary Cooper's reenactment in *Pride of the Yankees* works quite effectively. 2) John-John Kennedy saluting the horse drawn carriage carrying his father's casket as it passes him by on that November 1963 day. You can imagine the torrents unleashed when the adult John Jr. died in a plane crash and the footage of his famous salute was played ad infinitum. 3) Louis Armstrong singing "What a Wonderful World." Whenever I hear that song, the bittersweet pain of what it means to be alive comes to the forefront of my consciousness and leaks out my eyes. Now there's a number 4) Joey Ramone singing "What a Wonderful World."

Okay, there is a number 5. I really don't like to talk about this one. I guess I have to because I brought you along this far. I don't like to admit this one 'cause it may seem as if I'm dwelling in the past. I guess I am. You see I'm a teacher who is on sabbatical, which means I have the time to do things that I haven't had the luxury of doing, like dwelling in the past. Okay, here's the secret 5th tear trigger: I cry when I stand by Carla's grave behind the church in Titusville, New Jersey. That's about 60 miles from here. It's where she's from, past Trenton, next to Pennington, down the turnpike. And where she is. Behind the church. For nineteen years. I bring roses to put on her grave. Since September, I've visited a couple of times. Why? Because I have the time.

I can't decide whether to tell the story backward or forward. She died on September 26, 1983. She had been in the hospital all summer long. She shot 13 bags of heroin. She tried to kill herself. But she didn't die. At first. Her then boyfriend discovered her in an overdosed heap and called the ambulance. Donny was his name. They took her to Cabrini Medical Center. She languished for three months. She was getting better. She came to appreciate that her actions impacted others, that we cared about her very much, and that she had many reasons to embrace life. She understood that her father loved her. That I loved her always and forever. I visited her every day except for a couple of weeks when Elizabeth, my future wife, and I went on vacation. The only time I ever got mad at Lizzie was when she had the temerity to wonder aloud why everyone was so intent on keeping Carla alive, when she so obviously wanted to be dead. I didn't talk to Lizzie for two days, but when I thought about it, I couldn't stay mad at her. Who else would put up with a boyfriend who insisted upon visiting his ex-girlfriend in the hospital each and every day? Like I said, Carla was getting better. The tube in her throat was removed and she could talk. She thanked me for helping her father. She said she loved me. A few days before her release, she had a heart attack. And died. Like that.

2.

No, I don't want to tell this story backwards. It's not better this way. Drift back to 1978. Picture a college town. No, picture a decaying New Jersey industrial town moonlighting as a college town. That's it, you got it. New Brunswick, New Jersey, home of Rutgers, the state university. Visualize a block of student apartments just off campus. See porches and fresh-faced students sitting on the porches pretending to read weighty college textbooks. Picture a world wide open to a future as broad as a Montana sky.

Now picture me. Hopelessly alienated for no good reason. And I can't find my keys. I know my roommates Ray and Eddie are inside snoring away. The rumpled blackness of my clothing accentuates my hangover. Inflation battles unemployment in a pong match of epic proportions. Jimmy Carter is President. Disco is the rage. The Dallas Cowboys won the Super Bowl. Life sucks. I couldn't be happier. Laurie is standing on her porch next door. Looks like she forgot her keys too. Laurie and I usually smoke a late-night joint on her porch before I inevitably try to kiss her and she inevitably pushes me away and sends me on my way to my lonely bed next door. Damn, her ass looks good today. Must be the hangover. For some God knows why reason hangovers make me hornier than usual. I try a new tack. A rhythmic wolf whistle and a Barry White bass line, "Hey Momma, sure lookin' fine this morning." She turns around. Oh shit, it's not Laurie. It's maybe the most beautiful woman I've ever seen. At least talked to. She smiles. I blush so deeply I feel it in my fingers. "I'm sorry," I stammer, "I didn't mean to whistle. I'm not like that." It's okay she tells me, she just got back from Italy and she's used to it. I am blushing so much my breath feels red. She offers her hand, "My name is Carla, I'm moving in here with Nancy, Laurie and Cathy. Do you know them?" I nod dumbly, a deep shade of scarlet.

3.

Carla is here with me. Don't worry, she's still dead. It's a painting that my friend Patty made. She made it from a photograph I took of Carla as we were driving across the country. She's smiling at me. Her self-inflicted bad haircut looks as alluring as in real life. Carla never knew how to wear her beauty. So she mutilated it. Chopped bangs with gardening shears in the case of this painting. But the smile. A devilish Mona Lisa smile captured in a painting, but the smile is for me. I was there, I know. And Carla is smiling at me as I write and ride my exercise bike and watch MTV2, which is a new station on our cable system. Nowadays we call this multitasking, but I've always lacked focus, which might explain why I'm not more successful. I can stay focused if I have to, it's just that I see no great urgency to maintaining a focus. MTV2 rocks. It's much better than the real MTV. Carla would approve. Our cable company gave us this new station because they feel bad, no, let me rephrase that, because they are hemorrhaging money because they can't come to an agreement with the YES Network, the Yankees owned station. So people are pissed off at our cable system and are leaving in droves for the greener pastures of satellite tv. The video playing is a song called "Party Hard" by Andrew W.K. and it rocks hard and he can't dance a lick. I feel like punching my fist through the wall. I shake my head around but my locks don't whip around in sweaty glory. I don't resemble a bad boy anymore. My appearance is closer to that of a menacing middle-aged Bozo. I need a haircut. I pedal harder all the while pumping my fist along with "Party Hard." Thanks, Carla. Keep smiling.

But I digress. Carla and I were in love. I think we were. All I can say for sure is that I loved her as completely as my being would allow. Maybe it was obsession. Not the corny kind of obsession we see in perfume ads with delicately thin men in turtlenecks chasing after an impossible to please ice goddess in black cocktail dress, but the real gnawing in the pit of one's stomach, mind fogging tunnel vision love that I once was prone to. Carla lived next door to me on Guilden Street and I would find an excuse to visit her every day during the fall of 1978. If for some reason, I managed not to see her over the course of a day, I would lie awake all night, my mind spinning with yearning and jealousy. I may have failed to mention that I had a girlfriend at this time. Two actually. No, not Carla.

Her name was Angie. And Lisa. Angie was everything I might have asked for in a woman. She was a twenty-year-old Douglass College English major, half Irish, half Filipino, thinly built with firm, well-proportioned knockers, and what best can be described as a come-hither smile. She commuted between her home in Bricktown and Douglass. She often spent the night at my place rather than driving back down the shore. I loved her very much. I don't know if she loved me. She found me intriguing, no doubt about that. We met in our Beat Tradition course over at Douglass College where my roommate Eddie and I ruled the roost as wanna be beat poets. I was a challenge to her hippie sensibilities, I think. I worked hard for her. Maybe too hard. The amount of energy and brain power I had to expend just to get her into bed almost wasn't worth the effort. But it was. Angie was the master of the backhanded compliment. Lying in bed, famished from vigorous coupling, she would casually say something like: That was wonderful, I never orgasmed so completely before. It must be because your dick isn't too big like the other guys I've been with." Thanks, Angie.

And there was Lisa. She was in love with me. I might have loved her. I took advantage. I never officially broke up with her, I just lost her. Lisa lived across the street with Betsy and Sandra. Lisa was 19 when I met her. She came from Hackettstown, (which if you don't know New Jersey, is the serious boonies) and had a healthy farmgirl type of build to match her personality. If you need to visualize her, leaf through an old R. Crumb comic, you'll find Lisa there; big boobs, thick thighs, bubble butt, the living embodiment of earth mother. Lisa cared for me so much, bringing home food from the restaurant where she worked, typing my papers and straightening up the apartment that Raymond, Eddie and I maintained in a constant state of disaster. Lisa was loving, warm, comfortable. And she knew about Angie. Then Lisa discovered marijuana. She took to it with same warmth and relish she had previously taken to me. She exalted in smoke. She consumed, and was consumed, and finally lost herself in cannabis. Then acid. Then the psych ward. In retrospect, my fling with her was probably nothing more than a footnote in her more meaningful love affair with drugs. After a while she lost interest. Or I did. I forget.

4.

Sorry, Carla. Back to you, the subject of this twisted tale. Carla and I consummated our relationship the day after Christmas 1978. I had come back to New Brunswick from Dumont with two of my high school buddies, Mack and Phil. My Dumont friends loved visiting me in New Brunswick because they viewed the college girls as looser, wilder and infinitely more gorgeous than our hometown girls. Inevitably they would get drunk, and obnoxious, ultimately embarrassing me in front of my more sophisticated college cohorts. However, my college friends always had more patience for my Dumont friends than I did. Somehow they were viewed as strangely exotic in a working class sort of way. But on this particular night after Christmas, Mack and Phil's usual brand of charm was not warmly received. Perhaps the emotional residue of Christmas in Dumont saddled Mack and Phil with a desperate edge that came off as menace to those not familiar with the ways of small-town male frustration. Things started going bad after the eighth beer when Mack thought what the hell, he'd go for broke and proposition each and every female in the Bull Pen, with the wild hope of getting lucky. The Bull Pen was the bar where my college compatriots and I liked to drink, and where I had built up over the years a cache of good cheer. I could cadge drinks with the best of them, 3 dollars in my pocket could get me through the night.

Mack finally got around to Carla. I don't know what she said, but she rebuffed him amiably enough, keeping in mind I guess that he was my hometown friend. Mack came over to me. "So what's the story with you and Carla? Are you fucking her? Cause if you're not, I hope you don't mind if I dip my wick." All the embarrassment, frustration and pent-up yearning within me forged into a steely anger that centered in my knuckles. I punched Mack as hard as I could just as the jukebox changed songs and the dull thud of my fist meeting Mack's jaw reverberated through the Bull Pen. Unfortunately, just as Mack flew backwards, someone opened the door to enter. Mack tripped down the front steps and crumbled on the sidewalk with a splat that was matched by a crimson pool of blood spreading from the back of his head. I thought he was dead. Chris the bartender made a sweeping Ralph Kramden-like gesture for all the bar to see that I was 86'd big time. Phil, Carla and I went outside to survey the disaster. Sirens were approaching. Mack wasn't dead. But he wasn't all that alive either. Phil and I carried Mack to my apartment, where we wrapped his head with towels and deposited him on my bed. I took his car keys from his pocket before leaving. That night Carla welcomed me into her bed for the first time. I spent the next two years there and it was the happiest time of my life. For a while.

5.

I've done everything possible today to not write this story. I went to Sears to shop for a new washing machine to replace our recently deceased model, I caught up on my correspondence with people I've never met or care to meet, I cut our 12 x 10-foot backyard grass after taking apart and oiling our primitive hand powered lawn mower. And I thought about Carla. Our first night together didn't happen exactly as I said it did. Yes, I did punch Mack, and yes, I did knock him out. Yes, I did take his car keys, and yes, I did leave Phil in charge at my apartment.

After that, Carla and I went out. We went to a house party at Big Joe's house on Prosper Street which served as home base for the other partying contingent at Rutgers. The inhabitants of Big Joe's house called themselves the Prosper Street Irregulars and their hard partying frat boy style hijinks served as a yin to our artsy disaffected punk yang. Their parties cooked. But our presence made them cool. We played to type. Upon arrival, Ray, Carla, Malcolm or sometimes me, would go directly to the turntable and lift the Grateful Dead or Kansas album off and dismissively toss it aside. We'd inspect the album pile and settle on a Ramones or Clash album. Devo would do. Patti Smith was acceptable. Then the party would change gears and follow a trajectory of our choosing.

After the crowd finished pogoing to Devo's "Mongoloid," Carla put on Patti Smith's "Ghost Dance." This is one of the few songs I remember the lyrics to. I'll recite them for you: "We will live again, We will live again, We will live again…" Our crew; Ray, Malcolm, Eddie, Carla, René, Alice, Jane, and me, linked arms in a circle and danced a combination "Hora" and staggering minuet. By the time the song was over, Carla and I were making out and the turntable watch was left to Malcolm. I was lost in Carla's lips. Then, an inebriated whine, "Are there any lesbians here? I want a lesbian." It was Mack and Phil. I don't know how they found their way to the party, but sure enough Mack was conscious if more than somewhat bleary eyed and Phil was screaming from the bottom of his besotted soul, "I need a lesbian!" Mack looked at me and asked, "What're you doin' here? You're s'posed to be at college?" I could only smile. And dance. Phil said something to Carla that I couldn't hear. I smilingly nodded along. All of a sudden – whack– right between the eyes. Carla had thrown a nitrous oxide whippit canister and it broke upon impact with my face. Blood streamed from the bridge of my nose onto my face, my shirt, and the floor. Mack offered me his blood-soaked bandanna. Before I really knew what happened, Carla was upon me, wiping the blood up with her overshirt. Then she was kissing me, her face a bloody reflection of my own.

Then we were on the floor, the crowd dancing to "Rock Lobster" around us and on us. Some time before dawn we made our way home. Once again, I put Mack in my bed and Phil on the couch. I put Mack's keys on the pillow next to his comatose self. And I went to Carla's basement room next door. We spent the next 12 or 24 hours exploring the contours of each other's outer and inner selves. No doubt about it, we fit together nicely. If only that first night could have been extended for a lifetime…

6.

That was Elizabeth on the phone. She wanted to know something about the new washing machine we bought last night.

"Whatcha doing?" she asks.

"Writing."

"Oh, sorry." Her voice is hesitant tinged with reproach or maybe disbelief. "Whatcha writing about?"

"Life, my life."

She laughs. "Oh that's a stretch." She's being ironic. She doesn't know how right she is.

Carla and I become inseparable. I see to it. I spend mostly every night during the spring of 1979 in her bed. We eat together, study together, and drink together. Eddie, Ray and Malcolm become her best friends. Carla's roommates become my surrogate sisters. Life is clear and simple. Should have been. I see rivals for Carla's affections everywhere. If we're at a party and Eddie and Carla are off in the kitchen talking, I become suspicious. Is my best friend hitting on my girl? In the movie version of this story the soundtrack is blaring The Cars' "She's My Best Friend's Girl (And she useta be mine…)" Is she leading him on? Are they carrying on and everybody knows it but me? There's John Cooper, her totally tall, handsome albeit preppy ex-boyfriend. She smiled at him. What does that mean? Does she miss him? Do I measure up? I have always possessed the innate capacity to torture myself with pure unbridled masochistic zeal. An experienced psychotherapist would have a field day if she could ever get me on a couch, wading through the murky quagmire of my tangled deep-rooted insecurities. But that's not going to happen. That's why I write.

The question replays in my mind like an endless tape loop: Was my jealousy self-inflicted sabotage or was it justified? Looking back on events that happened over 20 years ago, the mature me can see how I should have behaved differently.

But I couldn't.

Carla moved in with Gwen and Nan in June. The new apartment was down the block from Greasy Tony's, the most notorious sub shop/ late night food stand in New Brunswick and maybe the world. When some uninitiated college student inevitably would complain about the color or texture of his pizzasteak, the hired help thought nothing of jumping from behind the bullet proof glass separating the workers from the customers with a tire iron or car antenna in hand. Seinfeld's soup nazi had nothing on the thugs working the counter at Greasy Tony's. Carla's place was 5 blocks away from mine, but it felt like 20 miles. Gwen was 26 years old and worked as Assistant Manager in the Rutgers book-store. She was a woman. Nan was a 25-year-old psychology grad student. She was a woman too. Carla and I bought a car togeth-er, a beat-up Toyota station wagon that we paid about a hundred dollars for. We went on vacation in the car. I forget where, but I know it involved a hotel. I remember the thrilling wave of maturity wash over me as I signed the registry Mr. & Mrs. Scott.

In September it was back to college, me for my fifth and final year, and for Carla one last term. Things started to change. Carla began seeing a psychologist at the Student Health Center who gave her pills that Carla said were to fight the urge to drink. Later on, Gwen let it slip out that they were to fight depression. I fancied Carla and me as the class couple; we were cool, second-hand clothes looked good on us, she was beautiful, and I was on my way to becoming a famous writer. We had it all, how could she be depressed? Oh yeah, I forgot to mention that Carla was a bad drunk. It's been said that God protects the drunks and the idiots. He sure watched over Carla. For a while. She never got slurring staggering sloppy drunk. Not like me. Quite the opposite, she became clearly lucid. Both of us shared one drinking characteristic; no internal shut off valve. Most people drink until they can't drink anymore and then they stop for the night. Not me, I drink until I reach a certain threshold, then I cross that threshold and drink more and more until I mercifully pass out, or get into trouble. Carla was the same. The difference being that when I'm drunk, I look and sound drunk. On certain nights Carla would say the most horrible things while looking me straight in the eye. "Don't look at me with those horny devil eyes and froggy mouth, I know what you're after and you ain't gonna get it. You don't just want my pussy, you want my soul too. You're lucky I despise beauty, that's why I let you into my warm and private bed. I told you I promised my soul to Mo when I gave him my virginity. You can pretend to possess me but all you're getting is second hand goods. Mo's waiting for me in heaven, and he's gonna get me the way I was at 17 when I was innocent and beautiful." The next morning she would recoil in horror as I recounted her drunken confessions. I never knew for sure if her true buried feelings were emerging during these inebriated unravelings or if I was hearing hallucinatory wordplay bubbling from deep within to the forefront of her consciousness. Either way, it was frightening.

She could be affectionate. And indiscriminate. Her affection was not always pointed my way. Too often I had to pull her off an all too comfortable friend (or foe). Her youthful philosophy professors constantly leered in her direction and repeatedly questioned me about our status as a couple. I got into more fights than I should have, though I've always appreciated the curative effects of a healthy row, especially while intoxicated, and double especially, with my intellectual superiors. One night I watched Carla glide elegantly through a closed plate glass sliding door. She walked right through it, glass shattering all around her. She never broke stride, delicately sitting down in a lawn chair, quietly sipping her beer as blood poured from a gash in her forehead. Over the course of our years together, my knowledge of first aid became an essential component of our relationship.

With time, my demeanor changed. I came to believe my role in life was to protect Carla from harm, opportunists, and fate itself.

Of course, this was an impossible task and she gradually came to resent my Jewish mother-like overprotectiveness. Yet I know that I saved her life on any number of occasions. Of course, ultimately I failed, but by the end I knew that only one of us was going to make it out of the relationship alive.

Predictably unpredictable. That was Carla. One time, after too many cocktails, I went into the Bull Pen bathroom with Henry, a drug dealer who dressed like a farmer, or maybe it was a train engineer. I know he wore overalls long after they were fashionable. Henry had a needle and a little plastic bag of heroin. He tried to shoot me up, but couldn't find a vein. He tried again and again. An hour later I had deep purple bruises extending over the length of both arms.

"Look, Carla," I shouted in drunken surprise across the bar holding up my bruised arms, "Look what Henry did to me."

A beer mug came sailing in the direction of my head. "Don't come near me, you selfish bastard."

With Ali-like reflexes I ducked as the mug smashed into the wall behind my weaving head. I felt a certain disjointed pride that my girlfriend was upset about my apparent self-destructive tendencies.

Wrong. I found out a couple of days later that Carla was angry that Henry and I didn't share the dope with her. I shouldn't have been surprised.

7.

Our band. Raymond and the Exploding Garbage Can Band. Looking at the photo album reminded me. I keep this particular photo album on the shelf with my most precious books. Away from our family photo albums. These pictures are from Before. Pictures of Carla. And me. There is a funeral mass card with a picture of a suffering Jesus with a glowing heart. It says: In

Loving Memory of Carla Ray Carlson, Born October 5, 1957, Died September 26, 1983. Wilson-Apple Funeral Home, Pennington, N.J. The priest at the funeral never mentioned suicide. I guess that technically speaking, Carla did not commit suicide. She attempted suicide. And was saved. And wanted to live. Then died 3 months later of natural causes. The heart attack. So they could bury her behind the church. Everything is all mixed together. Newspaper clippings, mass cards, love notes, photobooth pictures, fliers for poetry readings, a playing card from Lake Tahoe, photos of the band.

Somebody, maybe Benjamin Franklin said, "Necessity is the mother of invention." That was how our band came to be. Carla, Ray, Malcolm, Eddie and I were in the same English class; The Avant Garde in Modern Literature. It was the most fun class that any of us received college credit for and our long-suffering professor was at our mercy. Getting stoned for class became a biweekly ritual, only broken when we decided to digest mushrooms or mescaline as an added avant garde study aid. At the end of the term, Professor Bender gave us a choice – write a paper or submit a final project. No brainer. Sorry, Marcel Duchamp, Gertrude Stein, and Eugene Ionesco, but written analysis of your work would have to wait for a more sober time of scholarship. We came up with a band. Not any old band mind you, but… Raymond and the Exploding Garbage Can Band! The premise was simple – Raymond wrote the songs, played guitar, and sang. Billy Pidgeon, a School of Visual Arts classmate of Ray's girlfriend Alex, played bass in a sort of color by numbers way and generally looked too cool for school in his bushy black pompadour, precision cut sideburns, and tailored shirts. Carla, Eddie, Malcolm and I played upside down garbage cans pilfered from unsuspecting neighbors' front yards. For aural diversity, Eddie played bass garbage can with a severed broomstick, while Carla, Malcolm and I preferred banging with extra heavy gauge drumsticks. Back then, garbage cans were made out of metal, corrugated steel to be precise.

Amazingly enough, and probably because we looked and

sounded so different from other bands in the area, we got some gigs. We played the Sophomore class end term party and our entire Avant Garde class was invited. This gig counted as our final project. And wouldn't you know it, we sounded good. It also just so happened that a shipment of mescaline had just come through town and much of the party, including Professor Bender, was flying high. I can hear snippets of songs "I got a big thing in front of me/ they're all making fun of me. I got a big ugly throbbing purple thing, thing, thing…" Needless to say we passed with flying colors.

We played at Skillman State Mental Hospital and were much loved by the exuberant audience. Ray's old high school buddy Dave Remnick played second guitar that evening. His name may sound familiar because today he's editor in chief over at the *New Yorker.* After our fourth encore, the patients dutifully lined up and waited for autographs. We played at the Nuyorican Poets Cafe on the occasion of a beauty named Sugar's birthday. The audience stood about twenty feet away with hands firmly planted over ears and knitted brows not at all hiding obvious disdain. But Sugar liked us, and she gave me an inflatable yellow umbrella hat that I wore through our set. At the end of *Acceleration,* one of our most rockin' numbers, Sugar wrapped her arms around my neck and kissed me passionately with those full luscious lips which are forever tattooed into my daydreams. I pounded the drums with unabashed frenzy, lost in rock star heaven. We played the Cancer Marathon, a two-day Rutgers bacchanalia with the lofty aim of raising money to fight cancer, but more aptly remembered for setting the world record for most beer consumed in a single place over two days. You can look it up in the Guinness Book.

Raymond wrote great punchy songs and we the rhythm section created a wall of noise beating the hell out of banged up metal garbage cans. It was a formula that had to work in a punk rock avant garde sort of way. We played all over New Brunswick. *New Jersey Monthly* wrote a feature story about us, which was followed by angry letters from pissed off New Brunswick residents whose garbage cans had been stolen. We played at Mason Gross School of the Arts first annual end term party along with another fledgling punk band Liquid Idiot. We had fans. Then Ray got bored. Then we stopped.

8.

If Carla were not to die, would this story still be compelling, worth writing, or for that matter, worth reading? I don't know for sure, and I'm an interested party. It's been said of my people, the Jews, that we are endlessly fascinated by all things concerning the Jews. It's that way with me. I am forever fascinated by all things concerning me. Let's survey the possible storylines:

Carla goes on with her life. She works as a waitress in the same East Village restaurant she always worked. She falls in love with the ambiguously heterosexual night manager who also happens to be a coke dealer. After about 18 months of troubled marriage, Nick the husband is shot and killed in a late-night drug deal gone awry. Determined to turn her life around, Carla goes back to school and learns to be a graphic designer. She runs into her recently divorced former film professor Woody Cookson who still has the hots for her. They get married and move into a large house in Short Hills New Jersey. Once a year she communicates with me via Christmas card (an artist's rendering of their magnificent faux Tudor house) wishing me and my family the best. Along with the card is a computer printed recap of the year's events; things like Junior's hockey exploits, Hubby's job promotion, and Daughter's honor roll status. Left out of the year end recap is any mention of unpleasantness such as the September 11th terrorist attacks. I no longer know Carla. Worse than that, I no longer like her.

Or, she falls in love with a former punk rock star who has reinvented himself as a spoken word artiste. However, he has never shed his heroin habit. He turns Carla on to dope which she takes to with enthusiasm. The only punk rock junkie of his generation not to die of an overdose, he abandons her when she tests positive for AIDS. She battles on for a few years before succumbing a few days before my wedding. The punk rock junkie does not attend her funeral.

No, the only possible ending for this story is the real one. The tragic one. Anything else would be cruel. But we're not there yet.

9.

We moved to San Francisco after graduation. We loaded the beat-up station wagon Carla's father had given her as a graduation present, waved good-bye to Ray, Malcolm and Eddie and were on our way. We took along Bernie and Patty for the cross country drive we determined would be an adventure in the Jack Kerouac/Neal Cassady style. Actually, the adventure more followed the Charlie's Angels formula because Bernie and Patty were knockouts, and I had my hands full looking after three healthy fresh out of college babes as we traversed America. Here's a sample entry from my 1980 adventure journal.

6/19/80 – What a fucking day yesterday was. I woke up and Carla, Bernie and Patty were dressed. They said they were going on a hike. I took a piss and got dressed as quickly as I could. We decided on a medium sized mountain, though all of the Grand Tetons are tall. It had a fair amount of snow covering it. After about an hour and a half of vertical climbing, I started getting tired. We all did. Got to cut down on the cigarettes. Every 100 yards or so we had to rest. The altitude made it difficult to breathe. My shoes started hurting my feet, rubbing the heels raw. I never realized mountain climbing was so tough. I was way in back. Eventually I caught up to Carla. She was tired and her knees hurt. Bernie and Patty were up ahead determined to reach the top. Carla and I quit about 1000 feet from the top next to a snow-covered stream. I took off my shirt and Carla took off all her clothes and we played and slid and rolled in the snow. I took pictures. In about half an hour Bernie and Patty came sliding down our ridge on the snow like they were skiing, but without skis. I asked how it felt to be at the top. Patty replied

"It was a fucking ego trip, I could have stayed there all day." I wished I didn't smoke. At one point while Patty was leading, I saw her slip and fall in the mud and slide down out of sight. It looked like fun. Then Carla sat down and slid down. Then Bernie. Then me. It was too late by this time as I slid about sixty feet through coarse cold mud. What I didn't anticipate was the last part – a ten- foot cliff made up of large rocks. My ass must have bumped every one of them. I got up, covered head to toe in mud, ass sore as hell. We all looked like mud people, but at least the girls got some padding on their asses.

We cleaned ourselves up and drove to Jackson Hole. We decided to treat ourselves and stay in a hotel. We all stayed in the same room smoking lots of pot, taking baths and watching the one channel television. At night we went to The Million Dollar Cowboy Bar, a huge, crowded bar with the distinction of housing more cowboy hats in one room than I ever dreamed possible. Amazingly enough, nobody took off their hats in such a sweaty place. Maybe there was nowhere to hang them. Some hick kept asking Carla to dance, and even though she said no 3 or 4 times, he continued begging. Finally, he told her he'd buy her a beer if she'd dance with him and she said yes. They danced for about half a song jumping around and swinging each other like drunken monkeys. After the song Carla came back to our table and he bought us all a beer. Carla introduced Patty, Bernie and me to him, and I tried not to be jealous, but I was. He had a long scraggly beard and no mustache and looked like a goat. After our drink we went to another bar, a cocktail lounge type place. In the bathroom, a biker asked me where I got my jacket. I was wearing my black leather jacket. I told him I was from New Jersey where lots of people got 'em. He asked me if I knew a guy named Joey DiSalvo who was from New Jersey. When I got back to the table Carla was talking to some middle-aged guy in a crewcut. He told her that Clint Eastwood was at the bar. I looked around but didn't see him. Must have been in disguise. Patty was dancing with the goat fucker who had followed us.

10.

I never really wanted to live in San Francisco. But I had to get out of New Brunswick. Carla had finished school in January, but I had to hang in until May. Our lives became different, she was part of the working world and I was still a student. She worked as a waitress at Tumulty's Pub saving her money for our trip west. She was good at that. I could never save a thin dime. I continued life as a student working part time at the Rutgers University Press book warehouse, where I spent my time tutoring Jimbo, the none-too-slick warehouse manager, refining my whiffle ball skills, racing fork lifts and shipping out copies of John Ciardi's *Selected Poems*. I don't know how it happened because I had been vigilant in my jealousy, but Carla started seeing Woody Cookson, a film professor (maybe he was just an adjunct, but such distinctions were lost on me), whose claim to fame was that he was a member of Andy Warhol's inner circle a decade earlier.

Actually, I do know how it happened. Sometime around December, Carla realized she was pregnant. In retrospect, I should have realized that the pull out and cum on her belly method of birth control was not 100% effective. But so should she. I took care of everything, arranging for the abortion in the local women's health clinic. On the day of the procedure, President Jimmy Carter came to New Brunswick. I left Carla alone in her room so that I could see the President of the United States. As the Presidential motorcade zoomed by, I ran into Angie (remember her?) and we smoked a joint in honor of old times and the Presidential visit. One thing led to another and I wound up in Angie's apartment on the other end of town helping her drink a bottle of expensive Scotch that had been given to her. There was no reason to spend the night. But I did. Perhaps it was sheer perversity on my part, maybe it was one ignored woman getting revenge on her rival. All I know for sure, is I shouldn't have done it.

The next morning, I found out that soon after I left, Carla started hemorrhaging and her roommates Gwen and Nan had to take her to the emergency room. She was still in the hospital. Gwen couldn't even look at me. I never could explain to Carla why I wasn't there for her. She never asked. To make matters worse, about a month later, Angie called to tell me she was pregnant and that she knew it was mine. I dutifully borrowed the money (some of it from Carla), took our car, and drove Angie to the clinic for the procedure. The withering stares of the clinic nurses as I arrived with Angie were enough to render me impotent for the next 72 hours. While I don't think Carla ever found out what happened, she knew something happened.

Things weren't the same for the next couple of months. Carla finished school, worked in the restaurant, played in our band, took life drawing classes and retreated into herself. She met Woody. Actually he met her. I imagine guys have an instinct for when couples are going through a period of discord. Woody, a drinking buddy of Professor Bender was a fan of our band. He came into our lives as a friend, or shall I say customer. I was dealing small quantities of pot at the time and Woody would call looking to buy quarter ounces. Since I never was around (don't ask me where I was or what I was doing), I would leave the bag with Carla who would give it to Woody. I don't know exactly how I found out about them, but I think everyone knew about Carla and Woody before I did. And yes, for those of you sitting upon a loftier moral perch than I, that does make it worse.

One day, I went to Carla's apartment after work and Woody was there. He didn't leave when I arrived, and it didn't seem like he was going to leave. I sat there waiting for him to go. He didn't. He lit a joint and passed it to me. Time became interminable. It would not move. Finally, Carla said that she and Woody were busy and I could come back tomorrow. I laughed because I thought she was joking. Woody said something I couldn't, or wouldn't hear. I picked up the ashtray that Carla had made in pottery class and hurled it at Woody's head. It opened a bloody gash over his eyebrow. Carla was upon me, biting my ear. For the first time in my life I hit a woman, knocking Carla across the room. Gwen came out of her room where I guess she had been listening. I raised my fist to her. "Don't you fuckin' move." Tears were streaming down my face. I felt woeful and powerful at the same time. I turned my attention to Woody. "If you don't like the way I treat my woman, stand up and I'll kick your ass the way it deserves to be, you big pussy." I had been reading Bukowski for the past year, so I knew exactly how to behave in this type of situation. Thank goodness I wasn't reading Truman Capote.

11.

I worked from 2 to 10 p.m. and Carla worked days, so we didn't see each other as much as I would have liked. We often met at Vesuvios on Columbus Avenue (next to City Lights Books) for a mid-day liquid lunch. (I wonder if our initials are still carved into the back wall by the bathroom?) My job title was Assistant Cafeteria Manager, but I was more of a dishwasher/janitor than anything else. The daytime cafeteria staff was a gang of surly ex-cons who made no secret of their contempt of my white college educated ass, though contempt is not a word any of them would use to describe their feelings regarding my ass. Rudy, the oily cafeteria manager did not attempt to hide his loathing for my existence. He operated the cafeteria as his personal fiefdom, often taking young office workers into his office for "personal consultation" as he called it. The employees called it the United Filipino Bank, because the office staff was comprised predominantly of Filipinos. The office workers were a noisy lot, generally good natured, but prone to dramatics, particularly the males. I can't tell you how many slap fights I broke up during my time in the cafeteria. Another annoying habit of the clientele was their inability to master the finer points of microwave cooking. Apparently, fertilized chicken eggs are a delicacy in the Philippines. Yet, did they have to microwave them to the point of combustion, leaving me the job of scraping exploded chicken fetus parts out of the microwave?

The only non-Filipino workers who utilized the cafeteria were Rudy, Paco the cook, Willie the other cook, Manny the dishwasher, Leroy the security guard (by the way, the only white

Leroy I ever encountered), Mo the Palestinian janitor, who was as friendly as could be but loved to argue Mid-East politics (a pastime I still have no taste for), and me. I was not so shocked one day to open *The San Francisco Chronicle* and see a photo of Rudy, Paco, Willie, Manny, and Leroy being led away in handcuffs under the headline "Drug Kingpin Busted." When I got to work I was immediately promoted to Cafeteria Manager and told not to talk to the press. The President of United California Bank personally came in to the employees cafeteria to congratulate me. I was given a 25 cent an hour raise. The next day I quit.

12.

Literary San Francisco. A book I've always treasured. It's a large hardcover book signed by the authors, Lawrence Ferlinghetti and Nancy Peters. I remember the day Carla got it for me. It was my 23rd birthday, September 8, 1980. Gregory Corso and I were sitting in Vesuvios drinking pints of Anchor Steam Ale discussing why Gregory would not go with me to a San Francisco Giants game. To him the matter was cut and dry: "They sold us out man… they left New York 'cause they got no heart." Carla came running into the bar and pulled this book from under her sweatshirt. She gave me a kiss and handed me the book. "Happy Birthday Sweetheart!" The ink from Ferlinghetti's signature was still wet. Apparently he signed it for her and she walked right past the cash register, out the front door, and across the street to where Gregory and I were drinking. I was concerned. Corso was impressed. "Don't worry, that fucker makes enough money. He won't miss it." I borrowed a marker from the bartender and wrote my name in the back. I asked Gregory to add his name to the San Francisco literary canon, but he declined, saying he was probably already in the book. Sure enough, he opened the book directly to a page bearing his likeness. In the photograph, he's holding his young son Max. I'll always remember Gregory Corso this way, sitting at the bar at Vesuvios, his hand on an empty beer glass, looking at a picture of himself. His lower lip trembles, he grips the glass tighter, and I can see a type of sadness wash over him, as if the New York Giants are forever leaving him, as if he's afraid that Carla and I will now leave him alone, broke, and thirsty at the bar.

One of the better things about my stay in San Francisco was hanging out with Corso. I owe it to my best buddy Eddie in an indirect sort of way. Eddie spent the summer of 1980 at Naropa College in Boulder Colorado studying with Allen Ginsberg. He came to San Francisco flush with plans and ideas. As always, Carla and I were delighted to see him. Eddie introduced us to many San Francisco literary types who had summered at Naropa, including Paul Martin and Matthew Oldfield, two younger poets who had also studied with Ginsberg. These two were somehow taking care of Gregory Corso. I'm not sure exactly what taking care of Gregory Corso entailed, but it had something to do with regulating the amount of dope he was allowed to consume.

Gregory recognized kindred New York spirits in Carla and I, and for a short while we became partners in crime. Because we were not users, Gregory often offered to share his stash. It was only after Carla said yes for a second time, that Gregory started making himself scarce. Corso was however, the perfect mid-day companion as I whiled away the hours before work at the United California Bank. I would meet him and 4-year-old Max at noon at Grant Park. We would drink beer out of brown paper bags, or when I felt rich, we would take Max along with us to Vesuvios or Specs. Occasionally, Jack Micheline would stumble by and we'd share our brown bagged beer with him. I wish I could report that we had deep soulful conversations about poesy or metaphysics, but more often than not we talked baseball, ways of Gregory getting money (Micheline had many opinions on this matter), and the physical attributes of the women who passed us by with nary a glance. Sometimes Carla would pedal by, and we'd buy food at the market for Carla, Gregory, Max, and I to have a picnic lunch. Once or twice, Gregory left Max with us when he went out to score some dope. On the second occasion he didn't return for a long while. Carla, for once offended by someone's irresponsible behavior, said fuck it and rode off to work. Finally, after about an hour, Gregory came back bedraggled, looking as if he'd just been beaten up by the infamous Officer Biggarini (of Beat bashing fame). I was reluctant to leave Max in Gregory's charge, but he assured me everything was okay. I didn't see him for weeks after that.

Eddie also introduced me to another poet he met at Naropa, Dick Ramirez. For this I am not eternally grateful, and as a matter of fact this introduction serves as the lone blemish on Eddie and my 3 decades long friendship. I don't know exactly how things transpired, but Dick was looking for a place in San Francisco, so we rented him the spare bedroom in our apartment. Maybe we needed the money. I was dismayed by the response of our new friends Paul and Matthew after telling them that Dick Ramirez would be staying with us. Paul said, "In San Francisco? Don't let him stay, he's like cancer. He'll eat away at your peace of mind until there's nothing left. Tell him, Matt," Matthew reiterated the theme. "He's bad news I'm telling you. My ex-girlfriend and I got along great, we were going to get married. Then Dick Ramirez moved into the empty room in our apartment. Within weeks we were at each other's throats over tiny inexplicable things. Then the marriage was off." Jade, Matt's new girlfriend was more succinct, she burst into tears upon hearing Dick Ramirez' name. Uh-oh.

I can't pinpoint how Dick Ramirez ended our relationship, but he did. Upon first meeting him I was surprised because his physical appearance did not betray an aura of menace. Quite the opposite. My first impression on meeting Dick was one of pity. He was the classic nebbish, stoop shouldered, slightly balding, wearing thick glasses, head lowered while mumbling unintelligible salutations. Obviously, there was nothing to fear.

But he was always there. In our apartment. And he had some annoying habits. First of all, he was constantly leafing through gay S&M magazines and leaving them around. Carla once found one in our bed. I didn't care that much what Dick looked at, but when a friend would come to visit, and see *Fist Fucking*

Leather Boys on our kitchen table, it was a tad embarrassing. Dick ate only one meal a day, at twelve midnight. He usually began preparation at around 9 p.m., and used virtually every pot and pan in our kitchen to prepare his vegetarian feast. He never cleaned up after himself. That task was left to Carla or me, usually me, because for some reason I felt responsible for his presence in our lives. He could not utter a complete sentence, make that word, without clearing his throat in a phlegmy harumph, sort of like Billy Bob Thornton in *Sling Blade,* but not nearly as charming. I fully understand that Dick suffered a speech impediment, comparable to a stutter, but that did not make it any less displeasing to the ear. Carla was less understanding. "Spit it out," she would shout in exasperation, "I don't have all day." He just gave Carla the creeps. She refused to be in the apartment alone with him. Somehow, she too held me responsible for Dick's presence and it became an unspoken hobgoblin in our relationship. Carla would go out to a movie, or over to Matthew and Jade's place, timing her arrival home with mine at 10:30. Sometimes we would meet at Mabuhay Gardens (local punk club) or some other club to get lost in the music. Anything to not be alone with Dick.

Then Carla got pregnant. Again. Damnit, I should have learned. We should have learned. In California the procedure was different. Instead of the cutting and scraping favored in East Coast clinics, something resembling a piece of seaweed on a long Q-tip was inserted into the uterus causing cramping, contractions, and miscarriage. After a night of discomfort (and listening to Dick's never ending meal preparations followed by what must have been a game of paddle ball played in the solitary confines of his room) and a wasted Saturday spent lying around sweating and sleeping, Carla was back at work on Monday morning. But things were different.

The next weekend I took Carla to Lake Tahoe for her birthday. We arrived Friday evening at the Harrah's Casino resplendent in our freshly purchased Salvation Army threads. Carla was gorgeous in her Marilyn inspired black sequined cocktail dress, and I was none too shabby in my copper-colored sharkskin suit and matching two tone (red and black) roach killers. Okay, I'll admit that since childhood, my vision of fashionable elegance revolved around George Chakiris as Bernardo in *West Side Story*. But we looked good. I gave Carla $50 dollars to gamble with, the plan being to hang around the blackjack tables for a couple of days as the casino plied us with drinks. I was determined to hold my own for the night on $20 dollars. Wouldn't you know it, Carla was at my side in about 5 minutes, having exhausted her bankroll in a few large bets at the craps table. My first drink hadn't yet arrived. I hung in at my table for about 20 minutes, losing only 8 dollars, but it wasn't any fun playing cards with Carla standing next to me, bored and thirsty.

We bought a couple of bottles of wine and headed back to our room. During the next 40 minutes of drinking, Carla revealed to me how disappointed she was that we didn't even consider keeping the baby. All I could say was, "I didn't know." She said I was the only man she would ever have a baby with, and that she knew I would make a good father. Then she passed out.

13.

As I sit in at the white plastic table in our backyard trying to write, my nine-year-old son is yelling at me, trying to get the last word in an argument I wish I never started. I told him that I thought *Spiderman* was a much better movie than *Star Wars 2 – Attack of the Clones*. To further stoke the fires of his pre-pubescent soul, I told him that if I was single, I'd much rather have Kirsten Dunst as a girlfriend than Natalie Portman (Queen Amidala). I know, not exactly responsible parenting, but what can you really expect of a father whose idea of family time consists of us all sitting together on the dusty couch drinking Diet Coke, eating popcorn, and watching *The Osbournes?* Come to think of it, Kirsten Dunst looks like Carla. Then again, she sort of looks like my wife Elizabeth also.

Things started going bad after the second abortion, but they started going worse after Election Day 1980. I remember turning the tv on (back then, Election Day was a holiday) as we were getting ready to go out to vote, and Walter Cronkite announcing that Ronald Reagan had been elected our country's 40th President. I couldn't believe it, I hadn't even voted yet. I always associate the name Ronald Reagan with missed opportunities, and in a way, I hold him responsible for the course my life was to take.

The day after Election Day I was to meet Carla at some new club after work. I was to perform my poetry along with Gregory Corso, Jack Micheline, Dick Ramirez, Paul Martin, Matthew Oldfield, and bands like Wall of Voodoo and Oingo Boingo in a kind of countercultural San Francisco Arts Festival. I still have some posters and programs in a box in the basement. My bio lists me as performance poet, vending machine repairman, and original member of the seminal New York City band, Raymond and the Exploding Garbage Can Band. I was scheduled to perform at 10:30, directly before Wall of Voodoo was to take the stage. I smoked a joint on the 5 block walk from United California Bank to the club so that I would be in a proper California state of mind as I stood in front of the crowd. After finally convincing the doorman that I was indeed a performer, I proceeded to the green room with the notion of grabbing a beer or two before getting on stage. Upon entering the dismal backstage room, I noticed Jade sitting by herself weeping, and Carla and Matthew passionately making out in the far corner of the room. I grabbed two beers, chugged them down, and walked onto the stage to deliver a vitriolic, stream of consciousness rant that I only remember shards of. Bits of misanthropy, misogyny, homophobia, anti-California diatribe, and apocalyptic blood splattered imagery.

The audience loved me. Wall of Voodoo followed with a set of uninhibited fury. Two days later, I quit my job at the cafeteria. A week later, I took a plane home.

14.

Did I really leave Carla alone, far from home with Dick? I honestly don't remember. The memory of my last week in San Francisco has been reduced by time and maybe self-preservation to a blur. Judging from what I know of my character these past twenty years, the answer is no, I would never abandon Carla alone with Dick. I just wouldn't do that. But I can't think of any other possibility.

I am so sorry.

Eddie picked me up at Newark Airport. I settled in Hoboken with Ray, Malcolm, and Steve the Pharmacist in a raw brick and wood loft with grimy industrial windows. An overhead heater was so inadequate for the job, that it would shoot flames when starting up. The bathroom was an unpainted plasterboard box that only reached three quarters of the way to the ceiling. However, there was a lot of space. I was a guest, not a roommate, but my friends were more than gracious. They could tell things were not right with me, but it went unspoken. If there really is such a thing as a broken heart, mine was broken for sure.

Ray had a new girlfriend whose name was Cindy, but we all called her Cinful. She worked as a hairdresser at the E-Clips Hair Salon in New Brunswick, and she was cool in a townie working class punk rock way. From the moment we met, she acted as if I was important, and I was flattered to receive her attention. She's here with me right now. Her picture really. It's on the wall over my computer. She's sitting behind a small table littered with empty beer cans and liquor bottles. She has lots of black stuff around her eyes, her skin is pale, and her hair stands up in a 1980 New Wave do. She is wearing ripped fishnet stockings, a black sleeveless top, one arm draped demurely over her head revealing her underarm hair shaved in the shape of a lightning bolt. She liked to brag that she could drink milk fed college boys like Ray and I under the table. She couldn't. Like me, Cinful possessed no internal shut off valve. And like me, she was a sloppy drunk.

Often, when I went out with Ray and Cinful, he fell into the role of surrogate baby-sitter, whose job it was to steer a couple of juvenile alcoholics away from danger to the safety of home. Ray and I would come home from a night of club hopping one hundred percent broke, while Cinful would empty her pockets of a barrage of crinkled, wadded up dollar bills. While Ray and I were buying drinks, Cinful would be collecting all the loose bills left on the bar. "Where did all this money come from?" she would inevitably exclaim the next morning in mock horror. Ray and I could only smile.

I spoke to Carla on December 8th to tell her that John Lennon had been killed. She was basically indifferent to the news.

> "Guess what?" she asked.
> "What?"
> "I'm coming home."
> "Oh. Where will you stay?"
> "At the loft. Malcolm said I could."
> "Oh."
> "I'll be home the day before Christmas."

15.

Carla came to me tonight in yoga class. Yeah, it's true, I take yoga class. Why? The short answer is: because I can. The more complicated answer is: Elizabeth thinks it will be good for me to learn how to relax. I think I'm one of the most relaxed people I know. Whatever.

What I like best about our yoga class is that it's not at all pretentious, it's yoga with a Hoboken twist. The school is called Yogacabana and Nick, the instructor guides us through the positions with a new age baritone tinged with Hoboken intonation. He says things like, "Ya did your best, now fugget the rest" or "it's over now, if ya didn't get it, fugget it." I never was that flexible, but at 44 years of age, my lack of flexibility borders on the ridiculous. But I do my best. After about an hour of yoga poses we do something called Vedracina: Deep Relaxation. Nick talks us into a state of meditation, guiding us with soothing words. "Meditate on a word, a phrase, a face of a loved one, a calm peaceful place. Relax, you do not need to be on top of a mountain to do this. Focus on your mantra, surrender yourself to the mat. If you think you're not doing it right, then you're doing it wrong. It's simply spending time alone with oneself. Relax."

Okay, I'll admit it. I often fall asleep at this point. But sometimes I don't. When I don't, time comes to a standstill, or at least very close, and I guess I am meditating. To get into this meditative state, I begin thinking of a place. The place that gives me the greatest feeling of serenity is the 10 by 12-foot patch of green in our backyard that passes for a lawn. There's not all that much green space in our city, so this spot behind our house serves as a gateway to my meditative practice.

To be honest, I'm not always positive if I'm dreaming or letting my subconscious thoughts float to the forefront of my mind. It doesn't matter. I picture the green space of our backyard, then Carla sitting under the striped umbrella at our white plastic picnic table. She is wearing a blue silk tank top, a straw hat, and is stirring a colorful exotic drink. She smiles at me, not the smile of a long lost 25-year-old woman, but a 44-year-old womanly smile. She does not look like Kirsten Dunst, nor any other actress for that matter. She looks like herself. "Where have you been?" I ask, "I've been looking for you." She answers in song – Chet Baker's "My Funny Valentine," and her voice is Chet Baker's voice, and his voice is her voice. Unity: mind, body, spirit. Tears stream down my face.

I hear Nick's voice. "If ya didn't get it, fugget it." I sit up and stretch, determined to free my mind of spirits.

16.

Things were bad from the start. Carla was resolute in her desire not to lose her share of our mutual friends. The loft wasn't big enough for the two of us. Hoboken wasn't big enough for the two of us. She moved her sleeping bag into a far corner of the loft. We spoke to each other, but it was a forced stunted type of exchange. I was still in love with her. I didn't exactly plead, but I made my sexual needs clear enough. Okay, I pleaded. When I went out to the Mudd Club with Cinful and Raymond, a new companion would drag along. I was jealous that Carla was diverting Cinful's affectionate attention away from me. As might be expected, Cinful and Carla got along famously. Besides spurring each other on to new heights of alcohol consumption, Cinful introduced Carla to the joys of cocaine.

The unspoken tension reached a head some time in February. Steve the Pharmacist had brought home a couple of boxes of amyl nitrate poppers from the pharmacy where he worked, and was graciously sharing them with Ray, Cinful, Malcolm, Carla and me. These poppers were the real thing, not the fake butyl nitrate bottles like Rush or Locker Room favored in gay bath houses and sold in head shops. Nope, these were state of the art, heart stopping, hallucinatory, medicinal poppers. We were already drunk. The amyl nitrate brought a psychedelic edge to the party beginning with a pulse quickening, pounding of the heart, which took on a filling physical presence, expanding and contracting with the breath, the rhythm of life, before making its way to the brain and exploding in a rush of orgasmic rippling vibrations. I don't know exactly what happened, but when I came to my right mind, Carla was sitting on Ray's lap kissing the side of his face. I punched Carla in the jaw with all my might, knocking her off the couch and into the wall. She glared at me with pure malevolence. "C'mon hit me again if it makes you feel better. You can't hurt me."

"Hey," Ray protested as I hit him smack dab in the center of his nose.

This drill was well rehearsed. "If any of you don't like the way I treat my woman, say so now so I can kick your ass."

Nobody said a word. Ray's nose was bleeding. Carla's eye was turning a bluish purple. The situation was spinning out of control. For dramatic effect, I kicked over the coffee table overflowing with empty beer cans, grabbed my leather jacket and walked out. To this day, my biggest regret in life, is having punched Ray in the nose. He was, and continues to be, my best friend. He might also be the most peace-loving man in the world. Except for Eddie. The two best men at my wedding. Blood brothers.

I walked the entire twelve or thirteen miles through the freezing night to my mother's house in Dumont, arriving at sunrise, shivering and delirious.

17.

It didn't get better. I picked up my duffel bag of clothes and moved back in with my mom. A few days later, Carla moved in with her sister somewhere in Westchester. Thus begun the darkest 3 months of my existence. I still have nightmares. I did nothing but sleep for the first week of my homecoming. I didn't eat, watch tv, read a book, masturbate, or want to see anyone. Mom was concerned and insisted I see a doctor. He told me I had mononucleosis, which came as a relief, because had he told me I was suffering from severe depression, I would have believed him. I spent the next five weeks sleeping and replaying over and over again what had gone wrong in my life. By all counts, I had failed in every measure of manhood. I was 23 years old and living with my mother, I had no job, no money, and the love of my life was cutting a self-destructive swath that I was powerless to stop. I lost twenty pounds, reaching a post-pubescent weight of 115 pounds. If I just died quietly, faded into nothingness, I wouldn't have minded. The only thread that kept me alive was the thought of how much my death would devastate my mother who had already lost her first son to the nazis.

Carla tried to see me, but I wouldn't let her. I didn't want her to see me like this. She had moved to New York, got a job as a waitress, and rented a dingy one room flat on Ludlow Street.

One day I woke up to a wet kiss on my forehead that I knew to be from Carla's lips. She was crying. "Please forgive me for all I've done. I can't go on knowing how you feel about me. I love you, do you understand that? Even if we're not together, I'll always love you." I smiled, made the sign of the cross and said, "I forgive you. I absolve you of all your guilt. I will love you no matter what happens. Always and forever."

18.

Good loyal friends are what give us our worth. Family is what keeps us alive. Sometimes. Carla had a family, an older sister and two baby stepbrothers, who all looked like they were cast from the same mold; blonde hair, large green eyes, upturned noses and devilish smiles. My heart breaks again when I think of the precocious five-year-old twins running around at their sister's funeral, unaware of what was going on. They are men now, and they never really got the chance to know their beautiful, crazy, self-destructive sister. Ray and Andrew are their names. Wait a second, let me face my chair towards the wall. There are people I know in this cafe. I don't want them to see me crying.

Carla didn't get along with her stepmother. She called her manipulative and controlling. All I saw was a plain middle-aged woman who simply wasn't her mother. Her real mother died of cancer when Carla was 15 years old. Ironically, Carla's mother died in the same week of October 1972 as both Ray's father and my father. Sometimes, family or lack thereof is what bonds friends together.

Ray Carlson was a hardworking, unassuming man who loved his family dearly. After his wife's death, daughters Barbara and Carla kept his spirits up. They cared for their dad with daughterly love and devotion. After Carla left for college, he married a secretary in his office, a betrayal that Carla could not forgive. She often told me that the happiest time in her life was Senior year of high school when it was just her and her dad. I wonder if he's still alive. If he is, I wish him peace. As a father, I can think of nothing more agonizing than to outlive one's children.

19.

I got better. After a few months of convalescence, I moved out. With Eddie's help, I found a room in a rooming house in New Brunswick. I got a job as a forklift operator in an electrical parts warehouse. The rest of 1981 was spent making up for lost time. I hung out with Cinful and Eddie at the Melody Bar. As a matter of fact, Eddie and I made the Melody a popular place to hang out. It started at the Bull Pen. We were drunk as usual. Eddie put a quarter in the jukebox to hear a Talking Heads song. Somehow the record got stuck and wouldn't allow itself placement on the turntable. Eddie gave the jukebox a sharp kick. It just so happened that Chris the owner was behind the bar and he saw Eddie kick the jukebox. He made his exaggerated Ralph Kramden you're outta here gesture and Eddie was 86'd. About 20 minutes later, I received a phone call at the bar. It was Eddie. "Dean, I'm at this great old bar on French Street. These young guys own it and they say I should bring my friends. They say free drinks for anyone who arrives in the next half hour. It's called the Melody." In a few minutes me and about fifteen former patrons of the Bull Pen walked through the doors of the Melody to be reunited with Eddie. And sure enough, the drinks were on the house. There was no jukebox in the Melody, but a real live DJ playing music we actually wanted to hear. The Melody took over, quickly establishing itself as the most popular bar in town. Eddie and Cinful and I ruled. We never had to wait on line to get in, and we rarely had to pay for more than half our drinks. Until the day the Melody closed its doors last year, I was always a welcome guest.

If I had the wherewithal to make it to closing time, I usually had a choice of who to go home with. If there was no one to go home with, I just didn't go home. After months of lying around hoping to die simply to stop the incessant self-torture, I refused to sleep alone. Ray and I called it "The Power." This gift lasted about a year and during that year, I slept with more women than all the other years of my life combined. I harnessed "The Power" from all the malevolent self-loathing nestled in my soul, turned it around, and focused it outside myself. In other words, I was charming. And I refused to be alone.

Occasionally Carla came to visit. She was not about to let me lay sole claim to our mutual friends. Usually she'd stay with Cinful, or over at Eddie's place, but sometimes she spent the night in my room. And yes, we had sex. I couldn't help myself. I don't think she could either. Neither of us wanted to, but desire won out. Maybe it was memory. No, let me be honest. I don't think she really wanted to have sex, but my will to go at it was stronger than her will not to. I know it sounds horrible, but sorry, it's the truth.

Carla had come down to New Brunswick to attend a poetry reading that Eddie had set up at the Rutgers Student Center featuring poet Eileen Myles and punk icon turned poet Richard Hell. After the reading, at the party in the Melody upstairs lounge, I noticed Carla kneeling at Richard Hell's feet, her arm draped over his knee. Clearly she was his, and this was her way of telling me. I went home alone, destined to be tortured by inner demons who had been quiet as of late. For the next couple of months, Carla was Richard Hell's girlfriend living the life of a New York scenester. The life I had imagined for myself. It was also during this time that she started seriously using heroin, a habit that stayed with her for the rest of her life. It would be easy to say that after her initial romance with Hell, and dope, she became aloof and withdrawn. But it wouldn't be true. Carla had money. Don't ask me from where. Sometimes I'd meet her as she was getting out of work and she'd take me to an after-hours club. After scoring some dope, she'd hit me up, then herself. This was before AIDS. Barely.

20.

Ray and I moved into our apartment on East 12th Street between Avenues A and B in early 1982. The apartment, costing the princely sum of $350 dollars a month must have been the smallest space two men this side of Eastern Europe ever shared. It was located in the rear building of a turn of the century tenement. The bathtub was in the kitchen which was also the livingroom which served as my room. If you sat on the couch (my bed) and put your feet up, you could rest them on the bathtub. The couch took up half the kitchen/living room making it im- possible to open the oven door for cooking, not that we ever wanted to. I'm not sure if we were plagued by mice, or rats, but throwing out the glue boards holding the squeaking defeated rodents, proved a constant source of anxiety. After a while, Ray took to going at them with a hammer, but the consequences of this activity were somewhat messier and no less stress provok- ing. We used the shower curtain rack as our closet so personal hygiene had to take a back seat to necessity. Both Ray and I be- came maestros of the kitchen sink sponge bath. Since Ray had a girlfriend, he got the back room, a thoroughly unspectacular white sheetrock box that had no room for anything other than a double bed. The water closet was just that, a 3' by 3' room housing a turn of the century toilet that suffered water pressure problems. The Boy George poster above the toilet brightened the ambiance considerably.

Malcolm got me a job at Macy's, where I was promptly assigned to work in the china department. If the personnel department placed employees according to the principle of cutting down on the likelihood of workplace theft, they did well in my case, be- cause I had no interest in china whatsoever. What I needed was a new wardrobe, but it wasn't going to come from Macy's. Carla continued as a waitress, working in a trendy East Village all night eatery called 103, because it was located at 103 Second Avenue. As a waitress and sometimes bartender, she came in contact with an assortment of underworld characters and late-night creeps; musicians, clubbers, drug dealers, transvestites, prostitutes, and sundry actors, actresses and models climbing up and falling off various rungs of the career ladder.

Sandy was my official girlfriend at the time but she moved to Houston Texas to live with her brother. I can't remember why. I pledged my faith and allegiance to her, which was a noble ges- ture made easier by the fact that there is no place on earth lone- lier than New York City. The poet Robert Bly who grew up on a farm in desolate northern Minnesota once said that the loneliest year of his life was spent in crowded New York City. It's like being a freshman in high school. You exist, but nobody sees you. There's always someone better dressed, more polished, more mature, more handsome, more confident whom the ladies fall for. Never mind that us guys (or freshmen) can see these poseurs for what they are. It doesn't matter.

… So we started a band, a rather unconventional one at that. Cinful was our singer, but she couldn't really sing anything other than "Tears On My Pillow." I played guitar, but I couldn't really play guitar. We thought we'd slip past that hurdle by letting me play slide guitar in the tradition of Bryan Gregory from The Cramps, our then favorite group. Ray played bass, though he was an excellent guitarist, and helped out with backing vocals. Carla, who had been taking drum lessons from a friend of Richard Hell, played the skins. She had a new boyfriend whose name was Donny. His brother was a drummer in a local band and Carla could use his drum kit.

Our band was beyond dysfunctional. Poor Ray, not only had to teach us how to play our instruments, he had to monitor our drug use. Cinful and Carla were the worst offenders, but impressionable me was easily led. With the 3 of us high, practice was hopeless. We fought about everything. Starting with our name. First, we were The Amazing Skycocks, but Carla didn't like it and Cinful backed her up. I thought Rain of Terror was a good name, but Ray thought it was too hard edge for our actual sound. Ray and Carla liked pre-LSD, but I thought it somehow made us sound like we had small penises. Cinful and Carla seized my words and came up with The Small Penises, but I would have none of that. Finally, we compromised on The Love Searchers.

The only feminine presence in my life besides Carla and Cinful was the sales staff at Macy's. Being one of the few heterosexual salesmen on the eighth floor (home of Santa Land – read David Sedaris on this topic), I probably had my choice of eligible young bachelorettes, though I'm sure they assumed I was gay. Elizabeth worked the crystal department register across the floor from me. Mutual curiosity turned to desire which blossomed into love. We became an item. Our budding romance became the talk of the eighth floor. "It's like a Macy's Christmas story," sighed Curly the Mikasa salesman over lunch in the employee cafeteria. There were tears in his eyes. Elizabeth and I blushed, then laughed. When Lizzie and I got married two years later, pretty much the entire eighth floor was there to cheer us on. We were their star-crossed lovers who managed to elude our fate and escape the dungeon of retail sales. So many of them are gone now. AIDS.

The Love Searchers debuted at a club called A7, so named because it sat at the corner of Seventh Street and Avenue A. In New York, a simple declaration of address is often enough of a push to give an establishment a certain hip aura about it. We were The Love Searchers minus one. Cinful had left both Ray and the band to check herself into a Pennsylvania rehab clinic. Singing duties fell to Ray… and me. As you might imagine, most of my mental faculties were focused on not making my guitar sound horrible. Also, a strong melodious singing voice cannot be counted among my positive attributes. When Carla gingerly took off her overshirt, I was amazed to see deep blue tracks covering both her arms. I looked closer. Her eyes were unfocused. She smiled at me and her eyes rolled up in her head. Shit. Ray got us started with a count one…two…three… tinkle, plinkety, plink, plunk, plunk. Carla was hitting the drums with all the force of an anemic 6-year-old. "Play louder, more aggressive!" Ray yelled, but Carla was in her own groove, a groove that had nothing to do with the music we were attempting to make. "Sing louder!" Ray screamed, and I screamed out two songs at the top of my lungs. By the middle of my second song, the crowd had diminished by three quarters. Elizabeth was still there, watching intently from six feet away. It was at that moment that I knew I was in love. Ray sang a few songs and the two of us established something resembling a beat. Carla was a nonfactor. It was easy to tune her out because we couldn't hear her.

We played a couple more dates as a band, only because we had made the commitment previous to our on-stage meltdown. I saw Carla a few times over the next couple of months, but Lizzie had replaced her as the leading lady in my life. Carla moved in with Donny, up the block on West 12th Street, but I still didn't see much of her. I ran into Donny and he looked frazzled and tired, as if caring for Carla was wearing him down.

21.

May 23, 1983
Dear Carla,

Hi. I just talked to you on the street. You sounded confused. Drugs? I know dope takes the sadness and boredom out of life. And I know that at times you can get pretty damn depressed. After a while of doing dope, there's no more pleasure, you just need it to feel like a normal living human being. You sound like you're at that stage now. Dope is an artificial thing, designed to deaden the pain. It's better to be depressed sometimes and be yourself Carla, than to be a zombie. When we used to go out I always worried about your moods and worried that you would kill yourself. We don't go out anymore, but I still worry about you. Shooting heroin is a slow way of killing yourself. If the only way to get attention is in a negative way, then you're going to be a drag on those of us who care about you. When we're old and gray, you don't want to still think of yourself as a self-destructive little girl. You got to get a little tough. I know I'm preaching but I don't care. I also realize I got lots of problems myself, but that's not the point. I also know how down a person can get, because I've been there.

You should be saving your money for a drum set, not drugs. Which reminds me, your drumming sucks when you're high. Ray asked me if you were doing a lot of drugs. I said I don't know. But take my word for it, your drumming is really lackluster when you're high. You better stop doing dope now, because you're not going to amount to much of an artist. Besides not being able to afford art classes, you need to feel something to be a successful artist. Dope strips you of your emotions. All these drugged up pretty boys walking around the Lower East Side who call themselves artists ain't going to amount to much in the long run. Most of them won't even be around in another ten years. I could be wrong, but I doubt it.

You must feel pretty dumb by now for giving me the impression that you have such a drug problem that I need to lecture you about it. Please, don't kid yourself, you do have a problem. I know you don't have great self-esteem (neither do I). You are a beautiful, alluring, wonderful person. I need you around. If I never saw you again, I would still care about you always and forever. A part of you is imbedded deeply in my soul. For purely selfish reasons, I don't want any harm or sadness to befall you. I can't spend my whole life worrying about your moods and self-destructiveness. You have to make an attempt to be happy and take care of yourself. I'm sorry if this letter is sappy and stupid. Although I can be difficult to get along with, just remember you have a friend in me, and I'll always be around to lend a helping hand if you need it.

Love, (always and forever)
Dean

22.

Carla died on September 26, 1983. It was a Sunday and I was hungover. The previous night Lizzie and I had been to a dress up party at Malcolm's loft in Hoboken. At around 1 a.m. the lights went out, the power blew and we had to leave. The next morning, Ray called me at work. "I've got bad news. Carla's dead. She had a heart attack, she died last night at the hospital." I couldn't believe it. I had just seen her a few days earlier and she was doing better. She thanked me for helping her father and Donny. She told me she loved me. "Always and Forever," she said. The following day I had a job interview for a managerial position, or white flower, as we called it at Macy's. I failed magnificently, answering each probing question with a variation of "because I'm smart," or "I don't care." Needless to say, I didn't get the promotion. My days at Macy's were numbered.

The funeral was on Tuesday September 28th. I was a pallbearer. So was Ray. Malcolm was there. So was Cinful. And Steve the Pharmacist. Eddie was stuck in Boulder with only a bus ticket home. Gwen was there. Nan. Donny. His brother. Her sister. The twins. Her dad. And stepmother. And the priest. It was a Catholic funeral. It wasn't a suicide. She had attempted suicide, but died of natural causes. Heart attack. Heart. Break.

Her coffin was placed in a hole in the ground behind the church. Everyone went into the church to eat the chocolate funeral cookies, talk about the lovely weather, comfort Donny who was acting every bit the grieving widower, and to dawdle over the twins. I remained out back with Carla. I poured a shot of whiskey from my flask onto the ground. Maybe the dead get thirsty.

23.

I know that by writing this story I run the risk of forever losing the parts I choose not to tell. Maybe that's for the best. That's how it is with writers, what we put down on paper becomes the reality and all else gets lost in the ocean of forgotten memory. This is the story I had to write. Sometimes we must leave a piece of ourselves behind before we can move on. And I guess it's time to move on.

If this story was a Steven Spielberg movie it would end with me placing a single red rose on Carla's grave. But she's not Marilyn. And I'm not Joe DiMaggio. Or Arthur Miller. This isn't a movie. Instead, I continue to pedal my exercise bike, trying to burn away middle-age flab while scratching away in a spiral notebook and listening to Joey Ramone's newly released posthumous album.

> I see trees of green, red roses too
> I see them bloom for me and you

And I say to myself, what a wonderful world.

Bright sunny days, dark sacred nights
And I think to myself, What a Wonderful World.

BIG DICK

Sometime after midnight, George made a drunken lunge for Sandy on the stairway. She fell backwards and he fell with her, kissing her all the way down. Anyone unfortunate enough to be in the way was also knocked down. As everyone was untangling themselves George lay on top of Sandy kissing her passionately. Sandy liked George. She kissed back and they rolled around and over the bodies on the floor.

George overslept again. It had been a good night. George had drank more than usual, gone home with the prettiest girl in town and spent the night making love to her. George remembered every detail of their lovemaking. She was that good. George fell asleep on top of Sandy sometime around sunrise. The alarm went off at nine A.M. George slapped it quiet and slept for another hour. He awoke with a start. "Shit! Work!" Sandy was snoring. George's dick was still hard and inside her. He pulled it out and ran to the bathroom. George looked in the mirror and cringed. It was Sunday. Only assholes worked on Sundays. "I am an asshole," said George to the mirror. George noticed that it was difficult to urinate with a hard-on. It took an excruciatingly long time. George brushed his teeth, combed his hair and ran back into the bedroom to get dressed. George had a tough time slipping into his pants due to the fact that his erection had not subsided. "God, she was great," thought George out loud. He kissed Sandy on the cheek. She snored on. George ran across town to catch a bus back to the city. It was easy.

Sandy had come and gone. Same old story. George tried calling her a number of times but Sandy was cold and unreceptive. She said she had a boyfriend. She said she had to visit her parents. She said she had to wash her hair. George finally got the message after Sandy's boyfriend beat the shit out of him in the alley behind the bar.

George met Amy in French class. Living in the city was a lonely business. George signed up for French lessons at the local university figuring maybe he'd meet some people. Amy was a large breasted Jewish woman, with long brown hair and ten years on George. George had always wanted to make love to an older woman. Amy was the one. Amy had a thirteen-year-old daughter named Rita. While staring down into his French book George often wondered what the trauma of childbirth had done to Amy's pussy. Was it real big and stretched out? George could only imagine.

Towards the end of the semester a number of the students got together after a class and went to a bar. George was a bit apprehensive, knowing he couldn't hold his liquor and hoping he wouldn't make a fool of himself.

"What the fuck," thought George, "I can't let this drinking thing be no anchor around my neck. If I'm going to drown, I'm going to drown." The students in his class were a dull lot. Dotty, the middle-aged woman who was a slow learner and a constant source of irritation to George with her stupid questions, was drunk and giggling at Amy's horrific recapitulation of her disastrous marriage and divorce to and from Andre, an aging Italian hippie who sold used furniture in San Francisco and wrote beatnik poetry on the side. Other students were engaged in duller, less important conversations. George drank. Around midnight George's classmates started leaving. It was past their bedtime. Except for Amy.

"I want to party. Doesn't anyone want to go somewhere else, for just one more drink?" Amy asked. George responded quietly, trying his hardest not to upset the other students' plans: "I'd like to go. I know a good bar down by where I live. Drinks are cheap. It's where the cool people go."

Amy and George spent the next two hours sitting at a table in the back, looking and laughing at various funny hairdos and telling each other about their lives. Amy impressed George; she had done a lot. George felt like a dumb-ass kid. He liked to feel that way. The empty glasses piled up. After the bar closed, they walked to George's house. She leaned on him. He put his arm around her waist. "God," he thought, "this is easy."

George's apartment was a mess. It didn't matter. They went straight to the bed. George was excited. He almost tore off Amy's clothes. She responded in a similar manner. He kissed her all over, he mauled her breasts, he sucked her pussy, he licked her behind. She was wet and gooey all over. George got on top of her and she guided his dick into her. George was out of control. He wanted to fuck her brains out. "Easy," murmured Amy, "your dick is too big. It's making me sore. Take it slow, we got all night." George thought it strange. No woman had ever commented on the size of his penis before. George felt proud. He fucked her like he never had before, pumping quarts of semen into Amy before he fell asleep.

George planned to visit his ex-girlfriend Laurie in Arizona, for Christmas. He missed her and looked forward to the adventure of traveling. Something else began to occupy his thoughts. His cock actually seemed to be bigger than it was a few months ago. He looked upon his pecker with renewed interest. He named his penis, Duke. He dreamt of him and Duke ruling the world, reigning majestically above all of humankind.

After a fine meal with Laurie in an expensive Tucson restaurant they went back to her house. Once again, George was excited. He had not made love to Laurie in 2+ years and that was too long. As they were undressing Laurie let out a shriek: "My God what have you been doing, taking steroids?" George blushed. "I don't know what's happening. It seems to get a little bigger every day. I have a theory, I think it gets bigger with every woman I screw." Laurie kissed George like she never had before.

George's enormous penis was beginning to attract attention to its owner. George couldn't walk to the grocery store without women staring at his lower parts. George had to wear boxer shorts and tuck his penis through his right leg where it nestled warm and comfortably next to his knee. One day while returning from work George overheard two Puerto Rican girls talking. "Look at the little man with the big pecker," said one. "That's not his pecker," said the other, "he stuffs it with socks." "Looks like he stuffs it with a baseball bat," said the first. Women began finding George more attractive. He heard the whispers and felt the burning looks behind his back at the bar. Every night he met a new woman. George was quickly becoming a legend. He met women on trains, he met women on the street, he met women in the laundromat he met women at wrestling matches. George had his pick. He fucked as many women as possible, sometimes five or six a night.

George's monster cock was becoming trouble. He broke the jaw of a nineteen-year-old-punkette from New Jersey and was threatened with a lawsuit. He sent a washed out 42nd Street whore to the hospital with a ruptured bladder. George quit his job and went on disability. His schlong gave new meaning to the old high school phrase "third leg." George had to have expensive pants especially designed to house his gargantuan member. His cock was out of control. He was too big for any woman yet his penis continued to grow. George moved into a new apartment. His old one was too small. George's mother bought him a wheelbarrow for added mobility George purchased a basketball hoop for those times that the urge became too great and he had to relieve himself.

George became a recluse. His neighbors did his shopping for him. George turned to alcohol. It didn't help. His apparatus continued to grow. George discovered Jesus. He prayed continually. There was no deliverance. George got fatter as his days became less eventful. He spent his time drinking cheap wine and looking through old photo albums. George was losing it. Fast. He dressed his penis up in an old sweatshirt and pair of jeans and talked to it. It was his only friend.

George heard the sirens. He looked out the window. It sounded nearby. He smelled smoke, heard a commotion in the hallway. He felt hot. He tried to get up and out of the apartment. His penis was too heavy. "C'mon Duke old boy, time to get our ass out of here." Duke smiled at him. It was too late. Flames engulfed the building and the walls came tumbling down.

John Flynn and Pat Vallone were both twenty-year men for the New York Fire Department.

"That fire was a motherfucker, Patty," said Joe later that evening at the bar. "It's amazing we only lost two."

"Two?" said Pat. "I thought we only lost that one guy, that loner on the fifth floor."

"No," said Joe, "They found another one under the bed in the same room, but he was burnt beyond recognition."

Patty lifted up his glass: "May he rest in peace." They clinked their glasses.

"Amen," said Joe, "Amen."

A South Bronx Tale

"It's like the architects were hired to build a prison and then in mid-stream the order was changed: Build us a school."

One of my students came up with this theory. After an initial chuckle, I came to the conclusion that he was probably right. Samuel Gompers Vocational and Technical High School on Southern Boulevard in the South Bronx resembles a prison more than any public building, especially one housing youngsters, has a right to. There is a cement courtyard in the middle of the facility used by administrators to hide their cars from the public eye, two towers (sorry, no machine guns) that face the barren hostile expanse of Southern Boulevard between 143rd Street and 145th Street, locked side entrances (for teachers) and a heavily fortified front entrance complete with metal detectors, scanners, uniformed guards, and the occasional K-9 officer at the end of a very short leash. Once the late bell rings, all exits are electronically locked. This is the place I called home for 10 years of my teaching career. It is still the place some of my best buddies call home.

Occasionally while sitting in the dreary yellow room that is called the teacher's lounge, someone would remark in the middle of a particularly ridiculous conversation, "Wouldn't this make a terrific situation comedy?" As soon as those words escaped my comrade's lips a slow wave of depression would wash over me. It wouldn't make a good situation comedy at all. It wasn't that it was too depressing, it was just too damn drab and mundane. If there was a situation comedy that resembled our plight, it would have to be the 70s sitcom *Barney Miller*, for the sheer grimy civil servant world it humorously portrays. Like any good ensemble television show, we had our share of eccentric individuals.

Of course, the cast of characters over a ten-year period is ever changing, but featured players in our real-life sitcom would have to include the following teachers: Don Cordani the dapper but tough as nails Freshman English teacher referred to by students and younger staff members alike as John Gotti. Every year students (and an occasional teacher) would ask me if Cordani was connected. No matter how logical my explanation that a Mafia Don would definitely not want to spend his time pretending to be a freshman English teacher in a South Bronx high school, it never managed to convince. The cast would have to include Joe Parilli, Cordani's paisan, a rumpled old-school teacher who has thrown in the towel years ago, biding his time, surviving in the classroom on guile and a lifetime of experience, unable to retire because of gambling debts. Carol Steinberg, the personable and popular Art and Senior English teacher, looking at the other side of middle age, but still considered the babe of the department by virtue of her being the only female in the English Department. Andre Jefferson, a charming slacker who plays the race card to create a thoroughly uncomfortable understanding with students, whom he hopes will not squeal on him for not teaching (and consistently falling asleep at his desk). Bobby Notice, the good-natured Jamaican soccer coach who has an easy rapport with the younger students, though he lets his Seventh Day Adventist religious beliefs intrude upon classroom instruction. Pete McCourt, the kindly reading teacher who has a voice like Mr. Rogers, but whose temper boils over on occasion into fits of violent cursing and chair throwing. The word is out, don't even innocently get into a discussion with him about abortion. Pete is the most loyal and principled staff member; he will put his job on the line to protect a fellow teacher whom he believes has been wronged. He keeps a fifth of Jameson's in his locker, which he'll pull out during tense times, usually after one of his temper tantrums. Mike Nemorin, referred to as Captain Nemo, or simply Nemo by students and staff alike. He is the Chairman of the English Department and serves as a buffer between the mean-spirited Principal and the teachers in his department. He's not a very good classroom teacher, but possesses excellent interpersonal and political skills. Liked by all for his easygoing humanistic approach to education he's often at odds with the

Principal, whose job by all rights he should have. Then there's me; a hardworking, idealistic teacher, who shines in this setting by virtue of relative youth and lack of cynicism. Popular with students for being the "with it" teacher; the white guy who understands.

While we may not have the setting, nor the cut and dried plot lines for a successful situation comedy, we definitely have the characters. I most assuredly would trust these characters with my life. As a matter of fact: I did. Every day. For ten years. My mother always found it perversely ironic that I should wind up back in the South Bronx nearly 30 years after my family joined the great Jewish migration out of the Bronx and into the suburbs. While my existence was launched in the Bronx, my being was shaped in Dumont, New Jersey, a working-class town made up predominantly of Irish and Italian Bronx refugees. The teaching staff at Gompers resembled the populace of Dumont, a place I couldn't wait to escape from. Double irony on me.

Working at Gompers had its share of rewards. First of all, it was the only high school that would take me. Let me explain briefly. For the first year and a half of my career I taught at Automotive High School in Brooklyn. That's right: an entire high school dedicated to the task of educating our future auto mechanics and auto body technicians. I knew from the start that I had a gift for teaching English, though it took a while to get over the culture shock. For example, for the first two weeks in front of a class, the students kept repeating the unintelligible phrase "wheredeeame?" I thought it was some arcane bit of Ebonics that I was not privy to. Finally, during the first post-observation conference with my Department Chairman, she politely asked, "Where is the aim?" I was baffled, "What's an aim?" She patiently explained that every lesson has an aim, or goal, usually phrased as a question, and in New York City teachers write the aim on the board. Since that day, come hell or high water, I write an aim on the chalkboard each and every day, even if we're having a test or a guest speaker. Despite a few rough patches at the beginning, I could tell that I was a good teacher. So could the other teachers. A few of the older teachers got my ear and reminded me daily that it was a waste of my talents to be teaching English to a bunch of unappreciative future garage jockeys. Point well taken. I went out looking for a better situation. I landed a teaching job at Julia Richman High School in Manhattan after an interview that was more like an interrogation with the Principal.

That September (1986), when I reported to the school, I was placed in the charge of the Assistant Principal of Administration, a diminutive man with a pointy beard bearing a striking resemblance to W.E.B. Dubois, who took an instantaneous dislike to me. He asked me who I thought I was, going over his head, the New York City Board of Education's head, and the union's head, in going to the Principal for a job. I shrugged my shoulders and mumbled something about doing what I thought I was supposed to be doing. He told me that there was no position for me at Julia Richman High School. I asked if I could speak to the Principal. He told me that the Principal would be "predisposed" today. And tomorrow.

I went to the Board of Education headquarters on Court Street in Brooklyn. I sat in a pale yellow room for two days with a group of about 15 defectives who looked as if they just disembarked off the Voyage of the Damned. Finally, the person in charge of personnel placement agreed to meet with me. His name was Rufus Thomas, and I'll never forget the look of pure malevolence in his beady little eyes.

"So what prompted you to believe that you are larger than the New York City Board of Education's Bureau of Personnel Services?" he barked.
"Excuse me?" I stammered.
"You heard me boy, why did you think you could go over my head and interview for a job at Julia Richman High School? We have a system in place and we can't have peach fuzz faced newbies thinking they can get around our system, now can we?"
"I thought that's what I was supposed to do," I responded in an

all too thin voice.

"You thought? Do me a favor and don't think. I'm paid to do the thinking around here."

"What do I do now?" I asked.

"What you do now is get your sorry white ass out of here and hunt yourself down a job. You're so good making phone calls, setting up interviews, climbing the ladder. Place yourself! Good day."

I went home and started making phone calls. At this point we were three days into the school year. I called 40 high schools before anyone would see me. Samuel Gompers High School was number 41. Mike Nemorin hired me the next day, an act that I am eternally grateful for. On the spot I swore (to myself) allegiance to Gompers and Mike Nemorin; I would do them proud. At the time of my hiring, I was the youngest member of the English Department, a position I would hold through the next ten years of cutbacks, restructuring, lay-offs, job actions, and various budget crises. During my time at Gompers I worked under two Principals, three Bronx Superintendents, three mayors, five Chancellors, but only one Mike Nemorin. He, along with an admittedly burnt out, but good-humored veteran staff, made it worthwhile.

Because I worked hard, especially in the early years, and had a good rapport with the students, I had it easy. I helped Mike make teachers' schedules, assign rooms, plan lessons, talk to resistant teachers, and order books. Within a few years I was Mike's assistant, officially designated as Assistant Chairman of Humanities, which encompassed English, Social Studies, Languages (Spanish), Music, and Art. I only had to teach four classes and I got to pick which ones. Some teachers thought I was doing all the work and Mike was merely riding on my coattails. But that was far from the truth. Mike and I worked well together. What he really needed was a sounding board to tell him what bullshit would fly, and what wouldn't in regards to the rest of the department. In education, particularly in New York, there's a lot of unadulterated theoretical crap that's passed on down from the top to be disseminated and supposedly implemented by the troops (teachers). I was Mike's bullshit detector, and he was grateful to have me as an Assistant.

In short, I was needed at Gompers. I got along well with the students, and so few of them had two parents at home that I served as a sort of surrogate father to many, handing out sagely advice as well as welcome disapproval as the situation may have merited. I was also skilled at teaching for tests and consequently my students excelled on the English Regents Exam. Of course, this is not sound pedagogical practice, but in New York City only the bottom-line counts, and the bottom line is doing well on standardized tests. I was comfortable. I was well liked and respected by my fellow teachers. Even the Principal liked me. But I wasn't satisfied. I always wondered what kind of teacher I'd be with better students. Don't get me wrong, there were some exceptional students at Gompers, and some of my former students are already more successful than I'll ever be. The greatest satisfaction of my career has come from finding ways for my brighter students to live up to their potential. However, it was one of my brightest students who made me realize it was time to leave the Bronx. I'll tell you about how I saved his life. Maybe.

Ron Joyner was a bright, energetic, eager student who was in my Sophomore Honors English class as well as the Junior Honors English class a year later. Along with two other students, Harold and Derek, Ron was a year younger than everyone else in the class because he was in an accelerated Language Arts program in junior high school. He was not the most popular kid in the class, but I always chalked it up to his being younger and not quite as physically mature as the other students. Ron was a good student, not great, somewhat lazy, a good writer, and extremely well spoken. He was into Eastern philosophy and religion, and while he wasn't my first student who was into such things, he was certainly the most erudite on the topic. In fact, I could always count on Ron to make me look good at times when the Principal observed me. I remember one time we were talking about the conflict between fate and free will in a short story by Isaac Bashevis Singer and Ron started talking about yin and yang and the duality of the universe. The other students started questioning him about the concept and even the Principal got involved, and if I remember correctly, the Bronx Superintendent was also in the room and he got involved too. When the administrators left, they left satisfied in the knowledge that higher education was going on in the classroom here at Gompers High School in the South Bronx. That was Ron. He had the uncanny instinct to ask the perfect question to stimulate a lively class discussion. The students in class called him my boy, or Scott Junior, because he often paraphrased or repeated things I said in class and made them his own in order to impress teachers in other subjects. I didn't mind. In fact I was flattered. He graduated in 1992 or 1993 and I didn't hear from him for a couple of years.

The next time I saw Ron Joyner was on a tv screen some early hungover Monday morning in June. I nearly fainted when I turned on the tv and saw skinny Ron Joyner being led into a police car in handcuffs. He was arrested for a string of vicious crimes that shook New York during the month of June 1995. Apparently, Ron was the maniac who went on a rampage and beat one woman to death by pounding her head into the pavement in front of the dry cleaners she owned, sexually assaulting and beating a piano teacher in Central Park to the point of putting her in a coma, sexually assaulting a jogger near an overpass by the FDR Drive, and attacking a woman in Yonkers. If you think back through all the horrific headlines shrieking from the front pages of New York's tabloids, you'll remember that terrible week in June.

On the day of Ron's arrest, there were newspaper and tv reporters camped around the school. I had to run a gauntlet of cameras, wires, and beige trench coats just to get through the front door. That same morning, the Principal issued a memorandum telling staff members not to talk to the press under any circumstances. I spoke to other teachers who taught Ron and they all acted as if they barely remembered him, or as if they never knew him at all.

I knew that what Ron had done was as bad as any crime I'd ever heard of, but I couldn't deny his existence the way everybody else did. I just knew it wasn't right.

That afternoon I spoke to a reporter from the *New York Times* who was the only reporter dogged enough to follow me through my silence to my car. Finally, I told her to get in my car. I drove around the neighborhood surrounding my school telling her all about my former student. The next day my name and my words were in the *Times* article and paraphrased in the other newspapers. I was worried what the Principal would say, but fuck it all, there was such a thing as freedom of speech in this country.

As it turned out the Principal was not angry with me at all. She said my quotes in the paper were thoughtful and reflected well upon the school. Over the summer, the State District Attorney's Death Penalty Task Force visited me at home and I told them what I remembered about Ron Joyner. One of the prosecutor's told me that it was unlikely that they would recommend the death penalty because it appeared as if Ron Joyner suffered from a degenerative mental illness such as schizophrenia. He said that my testimony helped.

About a year later, there was a trial. The trial was a formality, it was basically understood that upon a guilty verdict Ron Joyner would receive life imprisonment with no chance of parole. I testified. It was unnerving walking into the packed courtroom and swearing upon a Bible to tell the truth. What was more un-nerving however, was Ron sitting at the Defense table looking exactly like he did a few years earlier, still the scrawny kid, not the grim-faced monster pictured in the news. When he saw me sit down, he smiled and waved "Hi Mr. Scott." I gave him a half a smile in return. I told the court about Ron's promise as a stu-dent, and about his diverse interests, and about his relationships with his fellow students. While I was testifying, Ron put his head down and began sobbing, at first quietly, then moaning loudly in an eerie wounded animal voice that filled the room. The judge threatened to clear the room, I think she may have ordered the jury out. For an eternity it was me on the witness stand and Ron Joyner, face buried in his hands wailing from the depths of his soul.

After my testimony, I left with a few other teachers who served as character witnesses. Outside the courthouse, reporters tripped over each other to get to us. That night my face could be seen on newscasts throughout the Metropolitan area.

At the end of the school year, I transferred out of Gompers, and out of the Bronx to A. Philip Randolph Campus High School in Manhattan. The Principal, who had always stood in the way of my earlier attempts to leave, signed my transfer papers. It was time for a change.

About a year after that, I was laying on my couch channel surfing on a lazy Friday night when an episode of *Law and Order* caught my eye. There on the witness stand sat a slightly balding, well intentioned, clueless English teacher testifying about the potential shown by a former student who had committed a string of heinous crimes. I flipped the remote. I couldn't watch.

Ginsberg Lives

The funeral started at 9:00 and I couldn't get there until 10:30 at the earliest. My buddies Eliot and Andy doubted I'd get in because the funeral was supposed to be for Ginzy's very closest friends and family, but the *Post* and *Daily News* had printed the address of where the service was to be held. I figured if I didn't get in, so be it, I'd stand outside with all the other grieving souls. It was at the Shamballa Center on 22nd Street and was to be a Buddhist service. I had no idea what to expect.

Why was I going to Allen Ginsberg's funeral? Because he was a friend, simple as that. He had been a friend for twenty years, definitely not the most exciting twenty years of his life, but twenty years that were virtually my entire adult life. Eliot Katz and I first met Allen in the fall of 1976. Of course, I'd heard of Allen Ginsberg before that. I'd seen him on the tv news chanting, marching, dancing, playing his strange black harmonium, exclaiming his poetry at various demonstrations, be-ins and happenings throughout my childhood in the sixties. In sixth grade I put a poster of him up in my room, not for any literary significance, but because he looked so cool and so strange with all that hair coming out of the stars and stripes of his Uncle Sam hat. I read about him in Tom Wolfe's *The Electric Kool-Aid Acid Test* which was like my Bible during my high school druggy days. As a matter of fact, I still have the book. Here's what Wolfe wrote about Ginsberg's encounter with The Hells Angels: "Ginsberg really bowled the angels over. He was a lot of things the angels hated, a Jew, an intellectual, a New Yorker, but he was too much, he was the greatest straightest unstraight guy they had ever met."

I read the poem *Howl* during my freshman year of college. *Howl* was a poem that did what no other poem could do; it spoke to me directly from the page. No interpreters were needed. In a matter of months, I was transformed from a biology major future doctor of America to a black clad too much attitude for so small a frame English major who wanted to some day be a famous writer. Also, during our freshman year at Rutgers, Eliot and I took an English class called The Beat Tradition in American Literature. It was taught by the most popular teaching assistant at the school, Bob Campbell, or Beat Bob Campbell as he was sometimes known. This class was like no other class I ever had taken. Each class session a different student would bring in a jug of wine for us to share as we debated the finer points of the Beat Generation. After a few weeks of wine fueled discussions, someone lit up a joint, and from that moment on pot smoking became an added stimulant to our daily discussions. We would stuff our denim jackets under the door so that the smoke would not waft into the hallway and the other classrooms. It was during these heady days of our "Beat Trad." class that I decided to embark on the career path of becoming a beatnik poet.

One fall day of our sophomore year Eliot and I were drinking beer on the front steps of our new apartment dumbly watching the Puerto Rican kids play kickball in the street. A black taxi pulled up in front of our house. A bald, bearded, slightly stooped man got out and began unloading boxes from the cab. It was Ginsberg! We got off our asses and helped Allen Ginsberg carry the boxes which were filled with copies of his father's book of poems to the house across the street which was the home of Kevin Hayes. Kevin was about five years older than us and the only real poet we knew. He was also the president of the Rutgers Gay Alliance, the group that was sponsoring Allen Ginsberg's poetry reading that night. We unloaded the books and promised Allen and Kevin that we would see the reading that night.

The poetry reading was more like a concert than a literary event. Ginsberg had a rock star aura about him, drawing the audience to his words, making the audience of about 500 people feel as if he were addressing each person individually. When it was over, people lit matches and lighters, and the star poet recited an encore and then another. After the encores were finished, I waited in line to talk to Allen Ginsberg and to give him a poem I had written that was inspired by his poem "America." My masterpiece was entitled "America 1976" and it was a godawful mishmash of teen angst, unrequited love, faux street wisdom, drug induced paranoia and recycled KISS lyrics. Ginsberg looked at the poem for about thirty seconds and said "The problem with this. . ." I cut him off. "Allen," I said, "put it away and read my poem when you have the time, then write me and tell me what you think. My address is on the back." What can I say, I was young, brash and stupid.

Eliot and I drove Allen back to his apartment in the city that night in Eliot's orange Chevy Vega, I guess because nobody else had a car, and maybe because he liked the idea of being driven home by two 19-year-old boys. We received a free guided tour of the East Village with Allen merrily playing tour guide and pointing out the historical significance of such non-sights as the Gem Spa, The Holiday Cocktail Lounge, and the apartment where Leon Trotsky lived before he went off to Mexico to meet his fate. We helped him carry his boxes of books up the flights of stairs to his apartment on East 12th Street. Allen asked us to sit down and join him for a cup of tea. I visually took in the landscape of his apartment thinking so this is what the life of a poet looks like.

About ten days after our meeting, I received a postcard. It's packed away in a box now, but it said something like this: ". . . to prevent falling into the dumb singleminded trap you fall into you must be mindful that each line should ring with poetry, imagery, panoramic vision, wordplay. As New Jersey bard William C. Williams states, 'No ideas but in things.' Your poem has moments, perhaps it could make a good Haiku. . . With Love, A. Ginsberg." At first, I was hurt, then I was angry, but when I thought about it, I was honored that a world-famous poet and beatnik would take the time out of his schedule to spend on me.

Over the years Allen Ginsberg and I maintained a friendship. A friendship that has had its ups and downs but lasted. Because of him and with him I read my poetry to larger crowds than I ever again could hope to draw. Allen once did a reading with Eliot and me at the Rutgers Student Center where he split the door with us 50/50, which was enough money for us to start our own magazine which we titled *Long Shot*. Allen has been a frequent contributor to our magazine, giving us previously un-published poems and photos and never asking for anything in return. Many of the friends I have today are friends I met because of Allen Ginsberg. The poems I've written often have Mr. Ginsberg in mind as the audience, whether to impress him or defy him. Some poet once said "when a man dies, a universe dies with him." He probably meant that each person has an almost infinite amount of associations and memories and feelings and thoughts within him or herself and when that person ceases to be alive those connections are lost. Allen Ginsberg's death must have left a sizeable hole in the universe.

The last time I saw Allen was about three months ago at a memorial poetry reading for Herbert Hunke. After the reading, Allen and I were going to share a cab to the Port Authority, he to catch a bus to Paterson to visit his stepmother, and me to catch a bus home to Hoboken. Eliot offered to drive Allen to the Port Authority and me home. We had a laughter filled drive across town at the expense of a mutual friend who had asked Allen if he'd listened to the compilation he produced of golf songs. Allen didn't understand the concept — songs about golf??? We spent the ride goofing on possible golf songs such as, "I'm Your Bogeyman," "Get Down and Bogey," "Take This Club and Shove It," "Putt, Putt, Putting On Heaven's Door." Somehow the conversation got around to death. "When my time comes," Allen said, "I want my body to lie in state at St. Patrick's Cathedral and I want all the lovers I've ever had who are still around to file past my coffin." "Hello Allen" I said, "first of all you're a Jew, and second of all you're a homosexual. Cardinal O'Connor's not going to let you have a funeral in his cathedral." He looked thoughtful for a moment, "Maybe then, St John the Divine. They're pretty liberal." We laughed.

Of course the funeral is packed. Over 500 people sitting on square red and yellow cushions listening to Buddhist monks chant. For his family and for all the Jews, *The Mourner's Kaddish*. Five hundred of Allen's closest friends in New York. People whose lives he touched in friendship. People who have stories to tell. There's Peter Orlovsky. There's Allen's 95-year-old stepmother. There's his brother Eugene. There's Amiri and Amina Baraka. There's Gregory Corso. There's Hettie Jones. Patti Smith. Anne Waldman. Lou Reed. Natalie Merchant. Phillip Glass. Laurie Anderson. David Greenberg. Hersch Silverman. Andy Clausen. Eliot Katz. And Me.

Mom

I am a good son. I am as helpful as I can be. I have trained my mother as well as any son has ever trained a parent. I don't need to say more about that. I am here for my mother in her dying days. And I don't feel guilt because I am here as she wastes away.

These are the last days. Today my sister and I decided we would put two morphine pain patches on Mom, one on each shoulder. The cancer has been eating away at her body day after day. She is slipping away and there is nothing we can do to slow the process of dying. As her body shrinks and shrivels away, her stomach grows distended as the tumor on her liver grows. She looks like one of those children from some famine stricken African country. . . sticklike arms and legs, hollow eyes and round swollen belly.

I am intrigued by the pain patches. They are filled with morphine that is released into your system over time. What would happen if I put a pain patch on? How would it feel? I ask my sister if she feels like trying out a pain patch and she looks at me as if I'm out of my mind. If I ever were to commit suicide, I think I'd do it the pain patch way, one on each shoulder, one on each side of my chest, another on my forehead, and hello sweet oblivion. But believe it or not, this is not about me.

Carol is my sister. She is here every day before work, after work, often deep into the night. If I were a Christian I'd call her a saint. Let's just say that Carol is one of the most truly good people I've ever come across. Thank God I'm not alone, because nobody can understand you like a brother or sister can. Nobody in the whole world has the same nutty parents. Carol and I are different in a number of ways. First of all, Carol is 13 years older than me and I guess you could say that she raised me as much as Mom did. Secondly, Carol has spent her entire life giving to others (myself included). I was always mystified by Mom and Carol's relationship, because it is like the mother and daughter switched roles. Carol has always been supportive of Mom, and often bailed her out of trouble. Sometimes I look at Carol's life and worry whether after all that giving there's anything left for herself. I'm not like that, I'm a taker, not a bad taker, but a taker nonetheless. I take gladly. If at all possible, I give what I can, when I can. Of course Carol feels guilty that we're not doing enough for Mom. I feel we're doing what we can.

Mom is the one who is dying right now in front of us and there really isn't a damn thing we can do about it. She's doing it, dying that is, with dignity; perhaps more dignity than she usually has in life. She doesn't ask for much, doesn't complain, and doesn't want to trouble us with talk of her fate. She's often in la-la land because of the patch, slipping in and out of consciousness. When she is conscious, she's been voicing a stream of consciousness narrative that rivals the best examples of Andre Breton's surrealistic writing. A couple of days ago she smelled a piece of soap that Jessica my niece, (her granddaughter, Carol's daughter, and yes, a woman in her own right) had given her and responded "this is the perfumed decadence of sprightly virgins awaiting deflowerment and defilement." Jessica and I looked at each other. Of course we asked her to explain herself, but Mom was done talking.

A few hours ago, while I was giving her some water, she stopped drinking, opened her eyes wide and said "you will always be my sweetheart, because you are such a gallant nazi fighter." I asked her if she knew who I was and she said "of course, you are my little boy Danny, my brave little boy."

I'm the baby of the family. Mom had four of us really. Her first born, Ernst was killed by the nazis at Auschwitz along with Mom's parents. Ernst died at six years old, so the two of us never lived on this earth at the same time, but his presence was felt.

Then there's Susan who is three years younger than Carol. Susan is autistic, retarded, schizophrenic and probably 3 or 4 other diagnoses that haven't been given names yet. She's been in mental hospitals for the past 38 years, since the day that I was born. When Mom dies, Carol and I will take over the responsibility of looking in on Susan for the rest of our lives. Again, Thank God there's two of us.

Six weeks ago Mom was okay. She was just plain old Mom. Then she started having dizzy spells and the doctor came to the conclusion that her diabetes was out of control. She was put in the hospital until the diabetes stabilized itself which it never did. Poor Mom had to learn how to test her blood and how to give herself insulin injections. She couldn't get the hang of it, so Carol learned how to give her injections. I am too squeamish and chicken hearted. Unfortunately, the doctors discovered lung and liver cancer. Mom has only been out of the hospital to come home to die.

My mom doesn't like to face her fate. She doesn't even admit she has cancer, at least by name. She calls it "the little cherry in her lung." She sort of thinks now that she's given up smoking it'll all go away. No, I guess she doesn't really think that. Probably the hardest part for me was taking Mom to the doctor, whom I knew was going to suggest hospice care. Mom was almost too weak to make it up the little step from the sidewalk to the doctor's office.

The doctor examined her and was supposed to suggest chemotherapy (Mom thought). However, the doctor told me in advance that Mom was too old and her cancer too far gone for chemo to do anything but cause more suffering. After examining my mom, who was not strong enough to unbutton her blouse, the doctor took me out of the room, closed the door halfway and said to me in a very loud voice: "if it were my mother I would suggest hospice care. It's not like you think. The patient can control their lives and end their lives with dignity." Of course he said it in a loud enough voice so Mom could hear.

Mom made the decision later that afternoon.

Hospice care is not like you think. In the olden days hospices were places where terminally ill people went to die. I guess they still are. But hospice care can be given at home. It means that no extraordinary measures will be taken when the patient's time is up. It also means that Mom has a fulltime live-in caregiver named Beryl who is from the Bronx who has become very important to all our lives. Beryl is as strong as Carol and I put together, and fortunately is sweet and seemingly has a lot in common with Mom. They really hit it off, maybe because they're both immigrants, maybe because they've both experienced heartbreak in regards to their children. One of Beryl's sons was gunned down right in front of their house in the Bronx. But Beryl, Thank God is healthy, and Beryl is here, and Beryl keeps Mom company, and Beryl tries to make Mom eat, and Beryl listens to Gospel music on some all-Gospel station I didn't know existed, and our lives revolve around Beryl. And I'll say it again, Thank God for Beryl. Hospice care means that Mom will die in her own room in her own house with her children nearby.

I understand that it's not a tragedy when the parent of a middle-aged man dies. Yet, when it comes to my mom, I still feel like a little boy. I'm not scared of death, I know what it is. Dad died when I was 15. I've lived long enough to lose more than my share of friends and loved ones. Dealing with a death is not as bad as everyone thinks. Sure you're sad, but it's not an overwhelming, debilitating grief. It's more like a piece of you is pulled out leaving a hole. With time the hole slowly fills in and the dead person's spirit, or essence, or whatever becomes a part of who you are. I guess a person doesn't have to die to become a part of you, but death fixes their presence within you. It gives form to a shadow. I believe. If Mom makes it through the night I'll be surprised. I think I'll take off work tomorrow. I should be around when the time comes.

So how does this story end? You know how it ends. I know how it ends. Even Mom knows how it ends. She dies. There are no miracles happening. A miracle at this point in time would be downright cruel. I don't go to work in the morning. A thirtyeight-year old man probably has no legitimate right to feel like an orphan, but we're not talking about rights here, are we? The light of dawn shadows the walls of Mom's bedroom as morning darkness becomes day. The clock on the kitchen wall doesn't stop ticking. It keeps right on moving. . .

Maestro

Let's start with Miguel's words:
Who ever thought it would end like this,
an old drunken Puerto Rican being led
by the arm down the path of eternity
by a Jew from New Brunswick?

This was written in my journal on the PATH ride home to Jersey on September 15, 2017, a few days after Miguel's 76th birthday. I had walked Miguel home from another drunken night at a bar on First Avenue. Somehow it fell upon me, as it often did to get Miguel home in one piece. There were many of these nights, most often (thank God) without me. Miguel opened doors in the literary world for me and my friends in terms of invitations, readings and publications, I've shared the stage with him and for him numerous times, but I most value those times when I had him to myself, or in a small group. I'm not sure the last time I saw Miguel, I believe it was early 2020 before the pandemic when I went to the nursing home with Nancy Mercado. His sister Irma was there. Miguel was in good spirits, full of projects that he had to know were long shots at best, including getting him out of there. I think that was the last time.

The first time was 1976 or 77. Rob Press and I emerged from our Ford Hall dorm at Rutgers after an epic bong-a-thon and wandered onto the lawn at Old Queens Campus to see a Puerto Rican man standing at a microphone between who I later found out to be Mikey Piñero and Lucky Cienfuegos. There was a pro-test about cutbacks to our state university and that man at the mic was Miguel Algarin incanting: "Mongo can not penetrate/ Mongo can only tease/ but it can't tickle/ the juice of the earth vagina…" His beaded necklace was jangling to the rhythm of his swaying. His eyes were closed and his voice was a plaintive call to the heavens. Our minds were blown.

Maybe a year later I found myself tagging along with Eliot Katz and Rob Press to the Livingston campus of Rutgers to sit in on their Modern American Poetry class with Professor Algarin. On that day Miguel did not show up. The students knew the routine, wait 15 minutes and then we were free to go. Another time he left a note on the door saying he was sorry to cancel class but he'd been called to New Mexico to mediate a prison riot. We later found out it was true. However, I did join the class for a couple of field trips to the Nuyorican Poets Café where Miguel introduced us to literary luminaries such as Willian Burroughs and Amiri Baraka.

During our senior year our band played at the Nuyorican Poets Café. Robert and the Exploding Garbage Can Band consisted of Rob Press on guitar, and Eliot, Bruce, Carol and myself playing upside down metal garbage cans pillaged from New Brunswick streets. Picture fifty glowering Puerto Ricans standing three feet in front of the band with hands firmly planted over ears. The two audience members who delighted in our performance were Miguel, and Sugar whose birthday we were celebrating. As a matter of fact, we were wearing yellow inflatable hats in honor of her special day. For some reason Sugar took a liking to me in particular and thought it would be cute for me to be banging on my garbage can with her sitting on my lap. Mikey Piñero on the other hand did not think it so cute. When I got up to go to the bathroom, he told me he was gonna cut me if I went near his girl again. After he left Miguel came over, "don't worry he's all talk, but he's harmless. And I told him you're gay." Gee, thanks Miguel.

A couple of years later, I'm living in the East Village and working as bartender/event planner at the Shuttle Theater with Miguel and Eliot Katz and we're all working with the two crazy Sardinian owners of the establishment. Once a week Miguel and I would go down to Houston and Avenue D to pick up 8 cases of beer and 4 one-gallon jugs of cheap wine. Miguel would watch me load the cases onto the hand-truck.

"Miguel, if we both do this it will go faster."

"Danny, you know I'm too old for that."

"Miguel, you're 42 years old."

"I like to watch you glisten with sweat; it lifts my spirit."

Miguel accompanied Nancy Mercado to our house in Hoboken a few times for Thanksgiving dinner. Caroline knew to have a fresh quart bottle of Absolut at the ready. Miguel, like Pedro Pietri always asked as part of the greeting "How's the family?" Miguel was a most appreciative guest, complimenting Caroline's cooking and hospitality. He usually brought along little gifts that he found on the streets or in the Port Authority. We still have a framed black and white photo of Marilyn Monroe somewhere in the house. Sometimes as the meal progressed, and the vodka bottle emptied, Miguel would get sentimental. I remember him and Mary Anne Thompson weeping openly to a Scissors Sisters song playing as background music during our meal. Of course, I gave him that cd which he thought "the most beautiful music in God's creation."

By sheer happenstance, Miguel showed up at Moe's, our Brooklyn Tech teachers' happy hour hangout in Fort Greene one Friday afternoon and stayed in his seat at the end of the bar for the next 8 months. Somehow after a couple of weeks he had all the teachers buying him drinks.

There were a few times I thought oh my God Miguel is dead and I'm left with the body, none clearer in my mind than the time I had to get him to an event honoring him at Hostos College and he was passed out drunk, no sign of breathing on his bed, while a young man I did not know sat crying inconsolably at the kitchen table. I had to drag him fully clothed into the shower to revive him, then strip him naked and dress him in nice clothes, then get him into a taxi for the event in the Bronx. I felt very much like John Travolta in *Pulp Fiction*. After much coaxing (and a couple of drinks) he got up on stage and lit up the room.

Miguel was always well aware of the people occupying the space around him, and he cared for those he loved, except when he didn't. He thought himself better understood as a Shakespearean character than a Nuyorican one. He was constantly thinking up projects for Eliot who was suffering from medical ailments, he repeatedly asked how Jack Wiler was doing years after he died and he worried about Nancy and how we could help her. All the while I constantly had to swat his hands away. He once told me it was my job to keep Steve Cannon quiet at the Nuyorican, but a few weeks later told me it was my job to escort him down the block to see Steve Cannon at Tribes.

Most people don't know that Miguel and Nancy sat on my couch for two improbable Giants Super Bowl wins over the Patriots though in his own words (well really Jack Wiler's) he didn't know dick about football other than Tom Brady is cute and he should throw to the tight end. After the game Miguel walked to the bus stop singing "We Are the Champions." He and I understood that he was the Giants unofficial good luck charm.

At the nursing home we talked about his next collection of poetry tentatively entitled *Dirty Beauty,* how it was just about finished and was going to be his best book yet, a conversation we had repeated for a good 15 years. I tried to entertain him as we sat in the dismal visiting room talking about past exploits and brief moments of glory. He grew impatient with my poor pronunciation as I practiced my Spanish by reading his poems to him. On one visit we wore ridiculous green hats at a Saint Patrick's Day party devoid of alcohol. Naturally, he asked me to go out and smuggle in a drink. I dutifully complied and when I returned with two airplane sized bottles, he was asleep in his wheelchair and I thought better of it.

How awesome it is to have him as a friend. The void he hoped to avoid is now filled with love. Miguel is irreplaceable, Algarin has taken his place among the immortals. *Camina suavemente por el camino a la eternidad, amigo.*

Death of a Poet

10.

I feed him chocolate pudding with a spoon.
"I kinda like this." He smiles, "for I am a mighty oak."
He looks at me suspiciously, "Who started the rumor about the fish?"
"Not me," I reply meekly.
"Just checking," he closes his eyes and drifts off.
The end is near. The morphine is working.
He opens his eyes: "Am I dying?"

9.

"What do you mean he doesn't want to?" I'm speaking to the A-2 nursing station at Golden Hill Rehabilitation and Nursing Center in Kingston NY, aka The Nursing Home.
"He says he's not strong enough, he just can't do it."
"But we paid for the medical transport van to get him here. We made all the arrangements."
I am flabbergasted. Raymond and I have spent the past few weeks organizing and cajoling Woodstock people to come to Andy's book party held at the Mothership, a performance space managed by Paul McMahon, Andy's former landlord. Over the past month Andy has repeatedly said the reason he's hanging in there is for the book party. How can he not want to? It's raining outside. No, it's deluging outside, but 25 hearty souls are here. Caroline is here. My son Casey. Raymond is more realistic and accepting about Andy's condition. I can't believe it. Three days later I agree that Andy will transition to palliative care. I give my approval over the phone. My voice is thin. Julia asks me to repeat myself.

Andy talks to Cassidy, his oldest son every now and then, when he can figure out how to get his phone to work. His other two children aren't particularly interested in mending fences. Andy hasn't been a good father, having abandoned his family long ago. The highest power in Andy's life is Poetry with a capital P. Cassidy and Andy make their peace. Each of his children will thank Andy in the coming weeks for "making them the person they are," words that I hope to never hear from the mouths of my own children.

8.

A routine sets in, a deadeningly boring routine. The routine centers around what's for lunch, what's for dinner, finger pricks, inspection of the stump, raising or lowering the bed, the change of bedding, the twice daily dose of morphine, the search for the remote, the search for glasses.

Andy is taken to the emergency room after slipping out of bed two nights in a row. Andy says the bed is tilted. They bring him a new mattress. Andy is transferred to a new room in the nursing home. Now, instead of a roommate who complains the tv is too loud during nightly watching of *Jeopardy* and *Wheel of Fortune*, he has a new roommate who spends his days watching game shows like *The Price is Right* with the volume turned up full blast. Andy, an avowed socialist, views this as a new affront to his dignity.

I bring him hot coffee on my weekly visits, which he is thankful for. Andy has complaints: The weekend staff is mean and not capable, the coffee is weak and lukewarm, the staff has hidden his glasses, the food is unacceptable for human consumption, they treat him like a child at times, they treat him like a prisoner at other times, the nursing home is woefully short-staffed, nobody tells him what's going on medically. The list goes on. Covid and RSV sweep through the unit routinely. On these occasions, Raymond and I seem to be the only ones wearing masks.

Physical therapy is put on hold because blood is not circulating in his good leg. Andy spends his days in bed, tortured by the game shows blaring from across the room. He no longer writes. He no longer reads, not even his own books which sit fresh and unopened on the shelf next to the bed. Raymond does his best, telling Andy about the many projects he is working on, and the various comings and goings of various Woodstock personalities. I am out of things to say. We talk about sports. We talk about my family. We talk about Buffy Saint Marie. I bring old friends like Michael Wojczuk and Robert Press to visit. They are impressed by how well Andy is doing considering the circumstances. I resent their optimism. I know better. Actually, I don't. Andy has surprised us before.

My patience begins to wane. I am annoyed when Andy is not dressed and upright in his wheelchair on days I come to visit. I appreciate a show. I get mad when he doesn't understand why I have to miss a visit to attend the funeral of my Hoboken friend and neighbor Aaron. It's hard to stay angry at Andy, always has been, but still, I wait a couple of days before calling him again. As I write this, it becomes memory. Things get lost.

7.

Somehow, we get two new books of Andy's poetry out at the beginning of 2024, *The Fabled Damned* and *Two Hearts Beat*. It is a labor of love, for both the publishers, and me. We think they'll give Andy reason to live. It does. For a while. On my weekly visits to the nursing home, we go over the manuscripts arguing over various spellings and odd capitalizations and seeming typos that arc obscure references that are crystal clear to Andy but no one else. He believes strongly in the Beat credo "first thought, best thought." I just want people to read the books.

I'm hungover, as is my wont on New Year's Day. Nevertheless, I drive 2 hours to bring Andy to a poetry marathon in Saugerties. Rhea, the physical therapist, whom Andy adores, supervises my training. I learn how to get Andy into the wheelchair, out of the wheelchair, into my car, out of my car, up steps, up a ramp. I ask

Rhea if I get a certificate for having completed the training. She looks at me like I'm crazy. It was a joke I tell her, but she doesn't believe me. People are surprised to see Andy as I proudly wheel him to the front row. A few look away from the white bandaged stump of his leg. I take a photo for Facebook. Andy reads a poem from the galleys of his new book. His voice is strong and fills the room. He gets the pages stuck together and continues reading from the middle of one poem into the middle of another. "Doesn't matter," he tells me later; "they heard my voice."

6.

Technology is a problem. Andy can't seem to work his phone. Raymond gets him a new one. Raymond gets Andy a laptop. He can't get his fingers to move the touchpad. Raymond gets him a tablet. Andy can't get it to turn on. I tell Julia, the supervisor that every nursing home should have a tech person to help the old people with technology, because not being able to use a computer or a smart phone isolates them further. She looks at me, "you're welcome to volunteer." I laugh.

Physical therapy is grueling. But Rhea pushes Andy. He's learning to walk with a prosthetic leg. His leg was amputated in October because blood wasn't flowing there. Diabetes. Raymond and I marvel how Andy has taken it in stride. The hard part for him is the phantom pain. The leg hurt before the amputation, and it hurts after it's gone. He asks for more painkillers. The doctor is reluctant. Andy finds a night shift worker who leaves behind an extra dose of morphine now and then.

I have access to Andy's health records. Raymond and I are astounded by his prescriptions: 180 dilaudids and 240 oxycotin each and every month. I ask Andy about this. "You have no idea the amount of pain I'm dealing with," he tells me, a sentiment echoed by every addict I've ever met. "What doctor would ever do this?" I ask Raymond later that day. Apparently, Andy has a friend, from back in the day who's a surgeon and just helping out an old poet friend who's in need. I mention that the drugs are for a 200-pound man, and that Andy now weighs in at about 135 pounds. "Hmm, he says striking a thoughtful pose, "I didn't think of that. Do you think maybe it's too much?" He thinks for another moment before adding "I don't take them all, Pamela has pain too."

Raymond and I work hard to get him in a nursing home, navigating and negotiating with the Ulster County social service system. We agree on Golden Hill in Kingston. I take Andy to Kingston where we meet with a social worker. Andy is bored by it all, somewhat passive as he allows me and Raymond to make decisions that will alter his life. I fill out page after page, form after form. We decide Raymond will have the power of attorney and I will be the healthcare proxy. Raymond is already a busy man, me not as much. Raymond lives in Woodstock; I live in Hoboken. We make a vow, at least I do, that we will be each other's emotional support partners. Over the next several months, when one of us is feeling pessimistic or overwhelmed, the other will be all good cheer.

5.

Andy is rushed to the hospital in an ambulance. Michael Platsky finds him unable to get up from under a dresser he's pulled down upon himself. Andy is yelling when Platsky walks in. He has been on the floor under a chest of drawers for hours. He's admitted to the hospital. His chart says "failure to thrive." I wonder what exactly that means. At least he'll be fed in the hospital. After a few days they amputate his right leg below the knee. As his health care proxy, I give my approval.

Andy can barely walk. It doesn't help that he does not seem to have a pair of matching socks, or shoes for that matter. He is content throwing on whatever right shoe and left shoe is laying on the floor in front of him. I'm embarrassed as he shuffles along in his mismatched shoes and socks at the supermarket or restaurant or drugstore. Andy couldn't care less. He's not embarrassed. He's never embarrassed. I've seen Andy Clausen weep, but I've never seen him blush.

Andy shows me his feet. They are black, especially around the heels. I'm not sure if they're discolored from the filthy floor or something is seriously wrong. I wash his feet with paper towels and dish detergent. The heals remain black. There are sores on his legs. "So," Andy says, "whaddya think." I tell him he should see a doctor.

His favorite restaurant in Woodstock is the Pearl Moon. He thinks it fancy; I think it a restaurant. I take him there after food shopping. He points to a parking space "See that space, that's where Pamela and I first fucked. Right in the car under that tree." I notice a tear making its way down his sunken cheek. Andy is at his best at the supermarket with the shopping cart stabilizing his broken stride. I can barely keep up with him as he cruises the aisle, picking up diet cream sodas and various "healthy" snack cakes that he calls porgy bait, a term he picked up in the Marine Corps. I take Andy to Walmart to get a new pair of prescription eyeglasses, the second pair since Pamela has died. I'm walking along thinking about a new poem Andy has read to me in the car. I think about his resistance to my telling him that he needs to spell thought correctly and not thot, when I hear a scream in another aisle. Somehow, Andy has wandered away from me and is now laying on the floor as a woman is screaming. I pick him up and dust him off reassuring the woman that he'll be okay.

Last night he almost burned the house down. He sleeps fitfully, drifting off in a narcotic haze at whatever time it hits him. At around 3 in the morning, he decides he's hungry and that he needs to eat something healthy, so he'll steam some broccoli. Paul his landlord who lives in the same building, known locally as "The Mothership" is awakened by a fire truck's siren screaming in the driveway.

Now, Paul is yelling, well yelling in that Woodstock way, which is more like a stern talking to. "We can't have this here. I live here too. You're gonna kill us all." I'm all apologies, though I have nothing to do with it. I just arrived. Andy sheepishly accepts responsibility "I'm sorry Paul, I don't know how that happened, it won't happen again."

I visit every week, furiously cleaning and trying to bring order to his apartment. I measure the passing time by observing the construction progress on the rest areas on the New York Thruway. I also measure time by holding my bladder until I get to the one open rest area located between Exits 17 and 18, about 30 miles south of Kingston, about an hour and a half into the ride. Mind over matter. Usually.

4.

Raymond Foye has stepped up big after Pamela's passing. He lives in Woodstock about half a mile away from Andy and Pamela. I know Raymond in passing. He is successful, more focused and serious than I ever will be. We are the same age, born in 1957. He looks in on Andy almost every day since Pamela's passing. Andy is appreciative. I am appreciative. I joke that Raymond is the most competent person in all of Woodstock, but I'm not really joking. He physically helps out in a real way as opposed to the emotional support in terms of healing thoughts or dharma wishes on Facebook that much of Woodstock offers. Michael Platsky comes over every other day to lend a hand and smoke a bowl with Andy. He lives a few houses down and his help is invaluable, though he likes to talk, which is perfect for Andy.

It's a week before I can make it back upstate. Andy has money problems. Anyone who knows Andy knows this is his natural state. He and Pamela are months behind on their rent. He can't grasp that Paul the landlord who has given them a sweet-heart deal on their apartment, might still want the same monthly rent now that Pamela is gone; in Andy's mind, his share of the rent, $500, is what the rent should be.

To say the condition of the apartment is squalid would be an understatement for the ages. The floors are black with grime that make your feet stick. Dirty clothes are piled over the floor, the bed, the couch, in the bathtub, everywhere. Pamela must have been doing the laundry at Peter Lamborn Wilson's while she was taking care of him. It seems as if the laundry hasn't been done since last year when he passed away. While Pamela's death came as a shock to Andy and much of the Woodstock community, a brief survey of the apartment reveals that things have been going very wrong for quite some time. Andy wears clothes that are ill fitting because he has lost so much weight over the past year, and they're downright filthy. When Raymond and I mention the condition of the apartment we develop a linguistic shorthand to summarize our feelings: "This is the Beat Generation." We laugh knowingly.

Dishes are piled high in the sink, charred pots sit on stove with food spoiling inside, rotting produce lines the shelves with bugs of various species crawling and buzzing around. Raymond and I set to work, clearing dishes, pots, expired foodstuff, unrecyclable clothing, donating books, clearing space. It's an insurmountable task. We look for outside help. None is forthcoming. Around Woodstock, it was Pamela who did these kinds of jobs for the sick and infirm.

Andy maintains a composting can in the kitchen. It's my firm belief that anyone over the age of 70 should be excused from composting duties. When I take the composting can out back and lift the lid, an ungodly collection of crawling and flying things make their way out. I gag as I shake the contents into the pile out back, then rinse the can with a water hose that doesn't seem able to muster enough pressure to complete the job. Andy calls this "country living."

3.

The damned car. The car is in Pamela's name, but Andy drives it more than she does. Technically, as next of kin Pamela's oldest child should get it. But Andy needs it, at least thinks he does. Over the next month, an all-out battle of wills resulting in Andy boycotting Pamela's funeral, and encouraging others to do so as well, which the greater Woodstock community happily does. The children spend extravagantly on Pamela's final farewell.

Hardly anyone attends. I find it unbecoming, and am embarrassed to be involved. Andy never drives the car again. Neither do Pamela's children. Michael Platsky winds up with the car with the promise that he will chauffeur Andy to doctor appointments and grocery shopping.

Her children plan the memorial. It's a disaster. I give money to the GoFundMe page. Andy is angry with me, "Why are you giving money to them when I'm the one that needs it?" They fight about the car. They fight about the memorial. Pamela's son leaves notes on Andy's desk. Things like "what goes around comes around" and "are you happy now, asswhole?" The daughter who lives in Florida, maybe the one in Georgia (I'm not sure), is the easiest to work with. She's the youngest in the family. Andy respects her the most. She writes gothic romance novels that are seemingly self-published.

Pamela's children arrive. They are grown adults in their 40s and 50s bringing with them grown adults in their 20s and 30s, the grandchildren. The children are from 3 fathers and are not particularly close to each other, though they share a postpartum grief in the loss of their mother, and a general mistrust of Andy. They come around the house poking through Pamela's stuff searching for what they can salvage. Nobody is helping, they are just wanting. Andy is passive, somewhat annoyed, but not being forthcoming about the circumstances of Pamela's death or his life with her. He answers their queries in one syllable spurts.

I feel guilty for doing the poetry reading while Pamela was dying. Andy lives for poetry. I don't. I know I'm not responsible, but somehow I feel responsible for minimizing Andy's concerns, falling into my default stance of "don't worry everything's gonna be ok." Andy depends on Pamela for most everything, much like he did a decade ago with Janine Pommy Vega, like he did 4 decades ago with his wife Linda.

2.

After a two-hour drive, I get to Andy's place. We're doing a poetry reading in Shiv's garden. I've read with Andy for parts of five decades, always making sure to read first, because nobody wants to follow Andy Clausen on stage. If Andy took the same care with how his poems look on the page with how they sound coming out of his mouth, he would be America's most celebrated poet. I have to pee. I knock on the door. No answer. I turn the knob, Unlocked. I find Andy sprawled on the floor blood covering his face. What the fuck? He's disoriented. "Andy, what happened?" He has fallen moments before. He's covered in blood. He's gaunt. I lift him up. It's easier than it should be, his hair is long and stringy. Bloody, He has a large gash over his right eyebrow. Sit him on the filthy couch. I get paper towels to clean him up. I go to the bathroom to pee. It's covered with blood and shit. I make sure not to slip. I need to get a bandage to cover the wound. I don't want to drive again. I walk to CVS, a 5-minute walk.

Andy is on the couch, holding bloody paper towels to his face. He's really frail. Almost skeletal. He's always been muscular, taking pride in his physique. Years of construction work, the working man's poet, strong, loud, proud.
"Where's Pamela?" I ask.
"They took her away this morning."
"Who's they?"
"The ambulance. It's her gall bladder. They took it out."
"Damn Andy. We don't need to do this poetry reading."
"Yes we do. Pamela wants it. She told me before they took her."

I get Andy the 50 feet from his apartment to the garden. I've done a good job bandaging his face. There's a decent crowd to see us. If only they knew how bad he looked just a little while ago. I read a long poem about my brother-in-law Leo's life and death. I never know what to read in Woodstock. Something about me just doesn't click with Woodstock audiences. I have my theories, which could be a whole essay unto itself. Andy reads a few poems by Pamela and a few of his own. He is weak but his voice is strong. Then the open mic. After I walk Andy back to his place, I go back to Shiv's and drink wine with him late into the night. I manage to clear a space for myself on the dilapidated couch, clearing books, papers, clothes, a toilet seat (?) before passing out.

I'm awakened by a loud whirring noise at 5 am. Andy is grinding beans for morning coffee. I look at my cell, "For fuck's sake Andy, it's 5 in the morning."
"I couldn't sleep, I was thinking about Pamela."
"It'll be okay. Caroline had her gallbladder out and she was as good as new in 3 or 4 days."

Pamela and Andy share a cell phone. It's with her. I rinse out a not too dirty mug and begin the process of waking up. I leave at 7 am, anxious to get home and take a shower, the smell of the apartment lingering in my nostrils on the drive home. At around 10 am I call Pamela's cell phone. No answer. 15 minutes later, I call again. At 11, I see the following message on Andy's Facebook page: "Now I have no working phone so I must do it this way. Last night the love of my life, the great poet Pamela Twining died in the hospital. You need to contact me on Facebook."

1.

I drive up to Woodstock blasting Orville Peck's "Daytona Sand" on the Thruway hoping not to get caught doing 85, happy to be reading with Andy Clausen and Pamela Twining in Shiv's backyard, officially dubbed the Shivastan Poetry Ashram. The last time I saw Andy was in October at a poetry reading he did with Pamela at Fox & Crow in Jersey City. Andy looked thin and tired. Somehow, he had set Pamela's poems on fire by reading them over a lit candle. It was Caroline who shouted across the room "Andy you're on fire." He wasn't, but Pamela's poems were, and a hole burned through the middle of the pages. After the reading, I insisted that they stay over in Hoboken and sleep on our none too comfortable couch. When Caroline got up at

6 a.m. they were gone. I love reading with Andy, it's always an adventure, as long as I read before him. Both Eliot Katz and I call Andy America's greatest living poet. I still believe that.

Danny Shot's *WORKS* was published in 2018 and his new collection *The Jersey Slide* makes its debut in 2025 also from CavanKerry Press. Recent endeavors include being an Associate Editor of *A Gathering of the Tribes* (2020-2023) and Poetry Editor of *Red Fez* (2018-2021). He was featured on the television show State of the Arts, NJ on the occasion of his book party for *WORKS*. Danny is a New Generation Beat Poet Laureate (2024 – Lifetime). Danny Shot was longtime publisher and editor of *Long Shot* arts and literary magazine, which he founded along with Eliot Katz in 1982 in New Brunswick, NJ. Check out his website: dannyshot.com

MORE ROADSIDE PRESS TITLES:

By Plane, Train or Coincidence
Michele McDannold

Prying
Jack Micheline, Charles Bukowski and Catfish McDaris

Wolf Whistles Behind the Dumpster
Dan Provost

Busking Blues: Recollections of a Chicago Street Musician and Squatter
Westley Heine

Unknowable Things
Kerry Trautman

How to Play House
Heather Dorn

Kiss the Heathens
Ryan Quinn Flanagan

St. James Infirmary
Steven Meloan

Street Corner Spirits
Westley Heine

A Room Above a Convenience Store
William Taylor Jr.

Resurrection Song
George Wallace

Nothing and Too Much to Talk About
Nancy Patrice Davenport

MORE ROADSIDE PRESS TITLES:

Bar Guide for the Seriously Deranged
Alan Catlin

Born on Good Friday
Nathan Graziano

Under Normal Conditions
Karl Koweski

The Dead and the Desperate
Dan Denton

Clown Gravy
Misti Rainwater-Lites

Walking Away
Michael D. Grover

All in a Pretty Little Row
Dan Provost

These Are the People in Your Neighbourhood
Jordan Trethewey

They Said I Wasn't College Material
Scot Young

Radio Water
Francine Witte

And Blackberries Grew Wild
Susan Mickelberry

Licorice Heart
Miles Budimir

MORE ROADSIDE PRESS TITLES:

Disposable Darlings
Todd Cirillo

Full Moon Midnight
Belinda Subraman

Innocent Postcards
John Pietaro

Cistern Latitudes
James Duncan

Another Saturday Night in Jukebox Hell
Alan Catlin

Abandoned By All Things
Karl Koweski

Ain't These Sorrows Sweet?
Lauren Scharhag

Gregory Corso: Ten Times a Poet
Edited by Leon Horton

She Throws Herself Forward to Stop the Fall
Dave Newman

We Don't Get to Write the Ending
Aleathia Drehmer

These Many Cold Winters of the Heart
Ryan Quinn Flanagan

Things You Never Knew Existed
Josh Olsen

MORE ROADSIDE PRESS TITLES:

Maze
Jennifer Juneau

Green Roses Bloom for Icarus
Hiromi Yoshida

Let the Scaffolds Fall
Shaun Rouser

Apocalypsing
Jason Anderson

Failing to Fall
James Griffin

Last Bacchanale
George Wallace

Thrift Store Jackets
Karl Koweski

www.ingramcontent.com/pod-product-compliance
Lightning Source LLC
Chambersburg PA
CBHW020118310726
48970CB00002B/691